TOBIAS

The Arcane Rebellion Book One

Written by Denis James

Legal Stuff

Text copyright 2024 by Denis James

ARCANE REBELLION names, characters, and related indicia are trademarks of Writing by DJ, LLC copyright Denis James

All rights reserved.

No part of this publication may be reproduced, stored in a retrieval system, or transmitted in any form or by any means, electronic, mechanical, photocopying, recording, or otherwise, without written permission of the publisher. For information regarding permission, write to Writing by DJ, LLC: writingbydj@yahoo.com.

This book is a work of fiction. Names, characters, places, and incidents are either the product of the author's imagination or used fictitiously, and any resemblance to actual persons, living or dead, business establishments, events, or locales is entirely coincidental.

Dedications & Acknowledgements

There are several people who I have to thank for getting me this far, but the person I need to thank first…is me. Thank you, to me, for finally having the courage to release this story that's been swirling around in my head for several years. And thank you for finally realizing that you, like Tobias, are not a waste of space. Thank you, to me, for removing myself from toxic situations and loving myself enough to put me first.

I need to give a special shoutout to Megan H., Kathryn D., Katie S., Ashley R., and Tracy B. for hearing this story first, giving feedback, and helping to make it as good as can be.

Finally, thank you to you. For picking up this book and entering this world with me. I hope you enjoy reading it as much as I've enjoyed writing it!

Much love,

Denis James

Table of Contents

Chapter One: Showdown at Jefferson High 1

Chapter Two: The Aftermath 15

Chapter Three: Bellwater Cottage 31

Chapter Four: Perfect Moments 44

Chapter Five: Confronting Shadows 53

Chapter Six: Substitute Teaching 64

Chapter Seven: It's Time to Duel 83

Chapter Eight: Gathering of Great Minds 95

Chapter Nine: Departure 107

Chapter Ten: Cruising for a Bruising 120

Chapter Eleven: Personal Attacks 131

Chapter Twelve: Best of Friends, Best of Enemies 143

Chapter Thirteen: Change in Leadership 156

Chapter Fourteen: Orders 166

Chapter Fifteen: Recovery 171

Chapter Sixteen: Trials of Leadership 183

Chapter Seventeen: Love Hurts 195

Chapter Eighteen: A New Beginning 207

About the Author 213

Chapter One:
Showdown at Jefferson High

It was a dark and stormy afternoon in a high school classroom overlooking a large parking lot and an array of trees. It was nearly the end of a long September day on a Friday afternoon at Jefferson High School. Football season was here, but there was a feeling of disappointment at the cancellation of the homecoming football game that had been scheduled for that evening. As it turns out, even high school sports are at the mercy of Mother Nature.

Sixteen students sat at their desks, occasionally looking up from their test papers just long enough to check the clock at the front of the room. Or spare a glance at their teacher, Mr. Tobias Thornfield, who was grading papers in the front of the room. There were less than five minutes left to go until the bell rang, signaling the end of the day and freedom for two glorious days. The test was difficult, the room was stuffy, and there was a general feeling of apprehension throughout the room.

Mr. Thornfield looked up from his papers to check on the students. He observed pencils scribbling as though their owners' lives depended on the outcome. He frowned as he looked at the faces of the students in front of him.

The students were unsure and nervous, and it couldn't be plainer that they didn't feel prepared for this test. Of course, this wasn't particularly a surprise for Mr. Thornfield. He had long since abandoned the idea that school would come as easily to his students as it had seemed to for him.

Mr. Thornfield was not an old teacher by any stretch of the imagination, but neither was he particularly young. While there were many peculiar things about this man, his appearance was anything but. A short, thin man with long, black hair, he did not seem to take very good care of himself. His hair was rather greasy and unkempt, and it was obvious he hadn't bathed for a few days. His clothes were a little dirty and disheveled, as though he had simply picked them up off the floor that morning and put them on. After a first glance, most people walking by would not give Mr. Thornfield a second one.

Despite his lackluster appearance, the students in this teacher's class seemed to respect him well enough. While his was a challenging subject (an upperclassman course in English literature) Mr. Thornfield was an excellent teacher. The students, and staff, at Jefferson High School all knew of his excellence. He would pass through the hallways, and students would show excitement at the upcoming lesson for the day, and staff would praise him for happenings in his classroom. When hearing uplifting comments like this, Mr. Thornfield shrugged them off; it didn't matter to him what students thought of him or his teaching style, and he cared even less what his colleagues thought. Only one thing mattered to him.

Mr. Thornfield was not an ordinary man. He had a secret, one that nobody at this school could learn until the very end of his tenure there. The organization he worked for had entrusted him to find new recruits for their mission. High school students were, of course, the most easily persuadable for this venture. They sought action, adventure, and excitement. But they were mature enough to recognize their own limits, unlike those irritating younger kids. By the time they hit college age, they were almost too mature; trying to convince a college student to join his organization was by no means impossible, but in his experience, they had a much firmer grasp on what exactly they wanted out of their lives than high school students did and thus were less likely to commit. For it was a lifelong commitment to Bellwater. You did not simply resign or retire; you were enlisted, and you stayed with the organization.

Mr. Thornfield checked his watch. The bell was due to ring in less than thirty seconds.

"Pencils down, everyone!"

There was a general murmur of anxiety rustling through the classroom at these words–the first words spoken in the classroom since Mr. Thornfield had passed out the exams forty minutes prior. Mr. Thornfield rolled his eyes inwardly.

"Calm down, everyone! We'll pick this back up on Monday. Give me your tests on your way out the door! If a test leaves this room, it's a zero."

At these words, the entire class breathed a sigh of relief. There were even some "yippies" thrown in there from a few brave souls. At this, Mr. Thornfield really did roll his eyes.

"Yes, yes, but do make sure you review more carefully over the weekend, yes?"

"Yes, Mr. Thornfield," several members of the class chirped back in happiness.

The bell rang thirty seconds later. The students packed up their bags hurriedly, threw their tests at Mr. Thornfield, and left to enjoy a weekend that would undoubtedly be filled with memories that Mr. Thornfield didn't want, or need, to ever find out about.

"Mr. Thornfield?"

Mr. Thornfield looked up; two of the students had stayed behind: Foxton Gray and Finnian Connor. Foxton was a tall student, a senior boy with flaming red hair and freckles covering his pale face. Finnian was a short boy, also a senior, with curly black hair and tan skin. The two boys could not look any more different, yet they were best friends. Or at least, Mr. Thornfield had assumed they were, as they were almost always together.

"Yes?" asked the teacher.

"We just wanted to tell you we think you're doing a great job!" exclaimed Foxton, beaming. He handed his test to his teacher, grinned at Finnian, and walked out of the room with his friend behind him.

Mr. Thornfield shook his head, not really getting the joke. But he didn't think much of it. He tossed the tests into a pile on his crowded desk–he really was an overworked teacher–and started getting ready to leave.

After all, it was the weekend for him, too, and he had plenty of stuff to do.

Foxton and Finnian were two of Mr. Thornfield's favorites. Every teacher, no matter who they are or what they tell you, is going to have favorite students. Foxton Gray was mischievous and had gotten on Mr. Thornfield's nerves on more than one occasion despite the fact that it was literally the third week of school. He was outgoing and popular, and earned good grades for himself, but the thing Mr. Thornfield liked most about Foxton was that he was genuinely very kind. He had met more than one popular student who thought they were way too popular for hanging out with students who were unpopular. But Foxton wasn't that kid; he would take the unpopular kid under his wing and build them up instead of tearing them down.

Finnian was one of those "unpopular" kids that Foxton took under his wing. Relatively quiet and not at all outgoing, Finnian was also the smartest kid in the room. Foxton–even though he got good grades–was not someone whom Mr. Thornfield would have considered book-smart. He earned good grades mainly from extreme effort and more talented friends, at least when it came to academics. Hence, Finnian Connor. A frontrunner to be valedictorian with his graduating class, Finnian had earned full-ride scholarships to several Ivy League schools.

Mr. Thornfield's thoughts were interrupted when a blood-curdling, glass-shattering scream pierced his eardrums. He looked up towards the door of the classroom, frowning. It was not unusual for him to hear strange, random noises coming from the hallway–high school students were unpredictable in that regard—but something about this seemed odd to him. He strode over to the doorway and didn't even make it before the one scream soon turned into two, and then several. Then, he felt something he never expected to feel in his classroom.

He felt intense heat and smoke coming from the first floor of the school. Students and staff alike were running, trying to get away from the source of it all, but it was no use; the heat and smoke were soon followed by red-orange flames. The fire was spreading quickly; it danced from one end of the building to the next, engulfing everything in its path. Desks, lockers, chairs, even people were swallowed by the fire as though they were nothing.

Mr. Thornfield hesitated, standing at the door to his classroom. The fire was spreading quickly…too quickly. A natural fire did not spread this fast.

A man materialized, seemingly out of thin air, at the end of the hallway where Mr. Thornfield's classroom was located, directly in front of Foxton and Finnian. The two boys, startled, jumped in midair at the sight of the man. This man was masked, covered head to toe in a black robe. Beyond the fact that he was of average size, it was impossible to make out his face or any distinguishing features. The man had not yet noticed Foxton and Finnian; he was facing away from them, looking at a small group of teenage girls who were trying to find a way around the flames.

The man laughed, a cold, merciless laugh that ran shivers down Mr. Thornfield's spine. Then the man snapped his fingers, and fire–pure, unfiltered fire–rained down upon the girls, engulfing them instantly. One of the girls screamed, but it was a short scream before it was instantly silenced. The girl had died a brutal, painful death.

Mr. Thornfield now knew what was going on…and he knew what he had to do. He had his orders: he was to protect the students he was preparing for the academy at all costs. The Bellwater Mages demanded that of him.

The man turned and noticed Foxton and Finnian, who were both frozen in terror, looking at the man. Foxton–the idiot boy–had pulled out his phone and started calling for emergency services, but Mr. Thornfield knew it was no use. Those boys were going to perish. Unless he did something to intervene.

So he did.

Tobias Thornfield snapped his fingers at the same instant that the man did. Fire, just like before with the girls, started to rain down upon Foxton and Finnian. But this time, the boys were not engulfed in flames. Instead, the boys were engulfed by a cloud of electricity that seemingly appeared from their pockets, protecting them from the flames. However, the madman who had cast the flames didn't realize their screams signaled they were alive, unlike those girls he had burned just moments before.

Tobias noticed the man was standing directly below a fully functioning light that had not yet been affected by the fire. He snapped his fingers again, and a bolt of lightning struck down upon the man who was casting the fire. He was sent flying and was knocked off the landing from the strength of the electricity, and slammed head-first to the floor below. Students screamed and ran away from the limp body on the floor below as he fell, landing hard. His body lay motionless on the floor.

The fire that was raining down upon Foxton and Finnian subsided. The boys went silent and looked around in disbelief; the school was still burning, and many people were still trapped. Tobias ran over to them.

"Don't ask questions!" he snapped at them as though that was their first inclination. He grabbed them both and pulled them closer to him. "Just wait for me…I'll be there soon."

Both boys vanished into thin air as suddenly as the man from before had appeared from nothing. Tobias looked around; his suspicion was that there was someone else who was causing the fire still to be found. His suspicion was proven correct when a man's voice suddenly carried from down below.

"Avery…Avery, what happened to you?!"

Tobias looked down below. The man whom he had knocked unconscious with a bolt of lightning was joined by two more men. One of the men looked vaguely familiar to Tobias, though it was impossible to tell any distinguishing features about this man from a distance.

"They must've overpowered him!" the unfamiliar man, who was slightly overweight and balding, screamed. He pointed towards a group of teachers running by. The teachers were instantly lit ablaze; they didn't even scream as they were engulfed in an instant. Another teacher nearby to them pulled the fire extinguisher off the wall, turned it on his colleagues, and sprayed it. The teachers were coated in a fire suppressant, but it did nothing.

Tobias vanished, and reappeared right behind the teachers who were ablaze. He had not been particularly close to any of his colleagues; after all, it was his first-year teaching at this school, and his teaching placements never tended to last very long. But he couldn't let them burn alive...he had to try and save them.

Tobias noticed a sprinkler up above where the teachers lay; the fire had not started the sprinkler system. He waved his hand towards the sprinkler, and water came gushing out of it as though he had just moved a giant boulder that was blocking its path. The water– which ordinarily would do nothing against this particular fire–was enhanced with magic, so it quickly put the fire out. But it was too late. The only thing left of the teachers were blackened, charred bodies that lay in the middle of the floor. Tobias sighed, and looked around for the two men, along with the unconscious man called Avery.

The smoke and heat were getting to be too much for Tobias. Everywhere he looked, students, teachers, even parents who had come running into the school trying to save their children lay on the floor, either dead or very nearly so. The fire alarm was going off, and he distantly heard the sound of fire trucks and ambulances, but he knew they would be too late. But if he could save just three more people...he would have all five new recruits for his organization.

And somehow, miraculously, he found them. But he

wasn't the first to find them.

The two men from before were standing in front of a group of students. The overweight man was holding the unconscious man Tobias had struck down earlier on his back. The students standing before them were two girls and one boy. The two girls were Lyra and Elena Wilkins; both of them were juniors in Mr. Thornfield's class and had just been taking their exams. They were identical twins, both with long brown hair and were the stars of the girls' basketball team. The boy was named Darian Keen; Tobias didn't know much about him, but he was a short, skinny, blond boy. He was not part of any sports or any club; as far as Mr. Thornfield knew, Darian was a total outcast.

The two men then spoke to the students. What they said made shivers run down Tobias's spine despite the fact that he was standing in a blazing building surrounded by smoke. It wasn't just what they said, however.

"You three! Come here, and we will take you to safety! You will be joining us."

He recognized that voice; it was Hunter Diaz. Hunter was someone who he had been searching for for a long time. He never expected, nor wanted, to run into him here of all places, especially not while there was a building full of innocent people being burned alive due to Hunter and his friends' actions. Tobias clenched his fists.

"What are you talking about? Why would we go with you? We don't even know you!"

"Girlie, you don't have much of a choice. Either come with us or be burned alive just like your friends!"

Lyra, Elena, and Darian didn't move. They were staring at Hunter, petrified.

"Is that how you want it? Fine!"

Hunter, a young, strong man of Mexican descent, with short black hair and black eyes, gathered an arm full of fire. The flames danced around him, obeying his every command. It didn't seem to harm him; on the contrary, it seemed to give him more life and purpose. He laughed, and Tobias knew what he needed to do. The flames lunged forward, directly toward Lyra, Elena, and Darian. Once again, Tobias disappeared and reappeared directly in front of the students.

At the exact same time of his reappearance, a tornado appeared in the middle of the hallway, in the space separating the men from the students. The tornado appeared seemingly out of nowhere and had been summoned by Tobias snapping his fingers at the exact moment he had reappeared. The tornado was quickly engulfed by flames, and then the flames were extinguished; the speed at which the tornado was blowing around was such that the fire was put out. Hunter and the other man stared incredulously at the tornado, then turned and spotted Tobias. Hunter gasped.

"Tobias!"

"What are you doing here, Hunter?" asked Tobias. He was livid; the last time he had seen Hunter, it had been under similar circumstances. But never did he imagine that Hunter would do something this destructive. The tornado died out, and they were now surrounded by heat, flames, smoke, and ash.

"I could ask the same of you, Tobias."

"I happen to work here. Or at least I did, till you burned the place to the ground."

"The place was a dump anyway. You're better off if you ask me."

"I didn't."

Hunter glared at him.

"So, what are you doing here, Hunter? Just burning down schools for the hell of it now?"

"I suppose I'm here for the same reason you are. Recruitment, right?"

Tobias didn't have time to react to this statement; twenty feet away, part of the roof fell in. Evidently, the building was starting to collapse from the flames. The English teacher could hear water being pumped towards the school; the firefighters had arrived on the scene. But it wouldn't do anyone any good.

Tobias made a split-second decision: he needed to protect these kids, no matter the cost. Aurora was counting on him. He and Hunter had history, but that was all it was at this point: history. He punched the air, and instantly, a powerful gust of wind smashed head-first into Hunter and the other two men.

The three men were blasted backward off their feet. Hunter smashed head-first into a trophy case and was soon pummeled by various awards that students from the school had won over the years. The other two men flew towards a nearby window, smashing it to pieces and continuing to soar into the grounds of the burning school, out of sight.

Tobias turned around to face the students behind him.

"Lyra! Elena! Darian!" he shouted towards them.

They looked at him, shock and fear evident on their faces.

"Come here!" he gestured, indicating they should get closer. "Quickly now!"

Just like with Foxton and Finnian, he pulled the two girls into a giant bear hug. Then they disappeared.

It was just Darian and Tobias now. But just then, the ceiling of the school collapsed right on top of them.

Dust, rubble, smoke, heat, and flames engulfed both Tobias and Darian. Tobias, with a quick flick of his wrist, was surrounded by six mini-tornadoes. The tornadoes blew the remains of the school ceiling away from him, and kept the flames, smoke, and ash at bay as well, though it did little for the heat. Darian, however, had smashed into the floor and after one quick scream, became lifeless and made no more movements nor sound.

Tobias swore; then he stretched out his arm, pointed at the spot where Darian had been moments ago, and waved his hand. Instantly, a powerful gust of wind blew the remains of the roof off Darian's lifeless body. The roof went flying right into Tobias's classroom. Tobias grabbed Darian, and vanished, leaving behind nothing but a destroyed high school and hundreds of dead bodies.

Chapter Two:
The Aftermath

Several hundred miles away from the burning high school lay a clearing in the middle of a beautiful forest. Mankind had seemingly left this space untouched for millennia; grass, weeds, and flowers flourished in this land as effortlessly as if the world's greatest gardener had made it his life's mission to keep this spot pristine. In the middle of the clearing lay a small pond, complete with bullfrogs, lily pads, and the occasional dragonfly buzzing over the pond. Nature was at peace with the world here; it was a quaint, comforting place, the sort of place one would visit to get away from the hustle and bustle of daily life.

That is, until two boys appeared out of thin air on the edge of the clearing.

The wildlife that had been enjoying the serene space– a couple of deer, some squirrels, and a fox–ran away instantly at the sight of two teenage boys entering their space, uninvited and unannounced. Foxton and Finnian appeared with looks of absolute shock and terror on their faces as to what they had just witnessed. They landed on the soft, pristine ground, hard, then quickly got back up with a rush of adrenaline.

"What the HELL just happened?!"

Those were the first words out of Foxton's mouth. He looked around, dumbfounded at where they had found themselves. Then he looked at Finnian.

"Hey…are you okay, man?"

Finnian looked as though he were in a state of shock. Of course, Foxton couldn't blame him for this; he, too, was still in a state of shock and panic from what they had just witnessed. However, Foxton knew something about his friend: Finnian suffered from extreme anxiety. He put an arm around Finnian's shoulder and gently lowered himself and his friend to the ground.

"Let's recap! Ok?"

Finnian nodded. Foxton looked away and pretended not to notice that Finnian's eyes were rather watery.

"We were taking a test in Mr. Thornfield's class…" "Then the school started on fire," croaked Finnian.

Foxton nodded. "Yes…but that was no ordinary fire. Did it seem really hot to you? And like it was spreading really fast?"

Finnian shrugged but didn't say anything. Their experience with fire up to that point was rather limited; the truth was, they had no idea how quickly a fire could–or typically did–spread. Firefighting wasn't something either of the boys really had an interest in.

"Those girls…" said Foxton quietly. He pictured the female students being engulfed in flames and dying instantly. He shuddered.

"Then I called 911…"

Foxton pulled out his cellphone. However, something was wrong; it was smoking and hot to the touch. Foxton frowned.

"Damn it! I think I'll have to get a new one."

Finnian looked at the phone and frowned. "The fire did that? Really?" He pulled out his own phone, which was also smoking and hot to the touch. He dropped it on the ground in surprise.

Foxton frowned too. "Now that you mention it…we didn't actually get hit by fire, did we?"

Finnian shook his head. "It seemed like we did…but I don't think we did. Something was protecting us."

Foxton bolted upright. "That man! The one who was laughing!"

Finnian looked startled at this. "The–the man who was laughing at us? In front of the fire? Where did he come from?"

"I dunno. I assumed he was a visitor to the school or a substitute teacher or something. I have never seen him before."

"But we hadn't seen him at all today either, so if he was a sub or a student teacher or something, we would've seen him before, wouldn't we? And didn't it seem like he just appeared out of nowhere?"

"C'mon man, he could've just come from around the corner…"

"You don't believe that, Finnian. You're not that naive."

Finnian sighed. "You're right. I don't believe that. But what other explanation is there?"

Foxton didn't answer. He stood facing the pond, lost in thought.

"Finnian…how did we get here?"

Just then, two brunette girls appeared not two feet away from them. The boys recognized the girls: Lyra and Elena Wilkins, twins, and players on the basketball team. The boys jumped at the sight of the girls, and Finnian stood up.

"What the hell, Lyra?!"

Elena was shaking, obviously having a panic attack. Lyra hugged her sister. "Elena, you need to calm down. We're safe now. We're safe!"

Elena took several deep breaths, and after a minute, her panic attack seemed to subside a little. The boys looked away from the girls during her attack and retreated farther into the woods. Once Elena had calmed down a bit, Lyra noticed the boys.

"What are you two doing here?" she asked, surprised. They had never spoken to Foxton or Finnian before; the boys were a year ahead of them in school, they had very few classes together, and they didn't play any of the same sports or have any of the same interests.

Foxton opened his mouth to speak, but before any words came out, two more figures appeared on the opposite end of the pond. The foursome turned to look at the two new figures; it was Mr. Thornfield, carrying a short, skinny boy who had dirty blond hair–though it seemed to be blackened. Foxton thought he recognized him, but it was impossible to tell. It didn't seem like the kid was moving or even breathing.

Mr. Thornfield laid the kid down on the grass in front of the pool. The students got a good look at him: his skin was blackened, and soot covered him head to toe. His body was bruised all over the place; it seemed like something had fallen on top of him.

Elena gasped. "Is that…Darian?! Is that you?! Oh no! What…what happened to you?!"

Mr. Thornfield turned to his four students.

"I need the four of you to listen to me very carefully," he said urgently. "We don't have much time. I promise I will explain everything to you, but first, we need to talk about your friend here."

He gestured toward Darian. Elena, who was sweet on him, started sobbing. "He's dead, isn't he?"

Mr. Thornfield nodded. Lyra and Elena embraced, sobbing silently into each other's arms. Foxton and Finnian looked at Darian; they didn't really know the boy, but they did feel a sting of pity for him and for his family.

"I need the four of you to stay back, please."

The four students looked at their teacher, dumbstruck. "What are you going to do to him?" asked Lyra suspiciously.

Mr. Thornfield said nothing. He stood there, his hands outstretched towards Darian. He was obviously concentrating very hard on the boy. He started waving his hands and arms around; it seemed as though he were trying to grab something from the air.

Suddenly, Mr. Thornfield seemed to have caught what he was chasing, and instantly flung his arms down towards Darian. A ball of white light fell from the sky and hit Darian's lifeless body squarely in the chest. Darian's eyes flickered open; he gasped for air, and then he screamed in pain.

Mr. Thornfield dropped to his knees in front of Darian and picked him up, embracing him like a father would embrace his newborn son. Bright, yellow light started to glow around the two. The four students looked in shock, amazement, and terror at the scene in front of them.

"What is…happening?" asked Foxton in amazement.

The four stood there and watched for what seemed like hours while Mr. Thornfield embraced his student. Then, as suddenly as it had started, the two broke apart. Darian stood up, eyes wide, looking from Mr. Thornfield to the surrounding clearing, and finally to the four students.

Darian looked at Elena and grinned.

"Hey!"

Elena walked up to him and slapped him.

"You DIE on me and the first thing you say is 'Hey'?!"

Lyra laughed. "Typical boyfriend," she teased her sister. Elena ignored her. She walked up and kissed Darian on the cheek.

"I'm glad you're safe," she whispered in his ear. He

kissed her back, feeling relieved.

"But what the hell happened?" he asked the group of students. "There was a fire, right? The school had a huge fire?"

"That's right," said Lyra. "And there were these two men—"

"Three," corrected Elena. "I saw an unconscious one fall over the balcony from the second floor."

"So three men," explained Lyra, "Who…started the fire? Then they told us that we'd better come with them, or else…"

"Or else what?" asked Foxton, interested.

"We don't know," said Lyra. "We have no idea who— or what—they were looking for. But it certainly wasn't us."

"But we got away from them," said Darian. "It seemed like they had been…blown away? By what?"

"Could the sides of the building have burned away and let the wind through?"

"That does not seem like something that would happen. And if it did, that would've been a really strong wind to blow away three grown men. Like hurricane levels."

"Then you two disappeared," said Darian slowly. "And…wait a minute! What happened to me?!"

The four students looked at him.

"When Mr. Thornfield brought you here, you were unconscious," said Elena gently. "It looked like a building had fallen on you. You were covered in burns, and your skin was blackened and peeling. I honestly thought you were a goner. But now…look at you! You're good as new. Mr. Thornfield…"

At the mention of his name, the five students started looking around for their teacher.

"But where'd he go?" asked Foxton. "He's the one who brought us here, isn't he? Where is he? What is he?"

Then, the students heard a gagging sound. It seemed to be coming from a nearby group of trees. The students jumped in fright; it sounded like somebody was vomiting profusely.

"Should we…go check it out?" asked Finnian quietly

to Foxton.

Lyra strode over to the trees and looked behind them as though she had no fear. Elena, of course, knew better; Lyra was always trying to show off for people, trying to get people to see how much of a badass she was.

"Mr. Thornfield?! Are you alright?!"

The other students ran over. There was Mr. Thornfield, a puddle of vomit on the ground in front of him, and he was leaning against a tree for support.

"I…I used too much energy…bringing Darian back to life. I need a minute, but I promise…I will explain everything to you. Just a minute. Go sit around the pond or something. I'll be fine."

The students went back to the pond, lost in thought. The idea that Mr. Thornfield had not only saved them from a burning fire, but also brought one of them back from the dead was an idea that was simultaneously alarming and wicked cool.

After a few minutes, in which the students just sat around the clearing checking out their surroundings, Mr. Thornfield staggered over to the pond. He sat down on the opposite side of the clearing from the students.

"Alright, I owe you an explanation, now don't I?"

Mr. Thornfield sighed. He had never really had to do this before; it was Aurora who usually did this, not him. But Aurora wasn't here, and it fell on him to do it this time.

"I suppose I should start," he said slowly. "With who exactly I am. My name is Tobias Thornfield. I was your teacher, but obviously, that will no longer be the case. I can assure you we are all presumed dead, or we will be at any rate. That fire…was no joke." He took a deep breath, and said quietly, "I have the power to control water, wind, and electricity."

The students stared at him in disbelief.

"Yeah, okay," said Foxton finally after a minute. "Like we believe that."

"Why do you think you and Finnian didn't burn alive when that man attacked you with fire? I used the electricity from your cellphones to save you. I used the water from the water sprinkler system to try to save your other teachers. I used the wind," he nodded towards the twins, "to blow away the men who were targeting the three of you." He indicated Darian at the end.

Lyra laughed. "You expect us to believe you? That's the craziest shit I've ever heard, and I've heard Elena's attempts at One Direction fanfiction."

Elena blushed redder than a tomato basking in the sunlight. "Lyra!" she said angrily.

Mr. Thornfield smiled weakly at the girls. "Don't believe me? I can prove it."

A bolt of lightning came crashing down in the clearing, mere feet away from where the students were sitting. The students sat bolt upright; it was a clear, sunny day. Where did the lightning come from?

"See that?"

The students frowned and looked at one another, then at Mr. Thornfield. Something was very, very wrong with this man.

"So..." asked Finnian nervously, "You made the fire happen?"

Mr. Thornfield shook his head. "I do not control fire," he said slowly. "I could, theoretically, use electricity to try to start a fire, I suppose, but it would not spread nearly as fast as that fire did. That fire engulfed everything, and everyone around it like it was nothing. The only thing that could've done that is magic."

"But then," asked Darian slowly, "What started the fire?"

"Not what, Darian. Who? Who started the fire?" "You mean, there are more of you?"

Mr. Thornfield sighed. "Yes, there are several of us, actually. I am part of an...organization. The Bellwater Mages. We are trying to continue the study of magic. Several of my colleagues are working at a high school not too far from here, Bellwater Academy. Teaching 'normal' school by day, teaching magic by night. Except me. I was to be undercover, recruiting more of you from high schools around the country in an attempt to bring you here. Truth be told, I have had my eye on the five of you for the short time I've known you. You'd be excellent additions to our school."

"But apparently, I am not the only one who thought so."

"There is another organization, known as the Arcane Rebellion, that we are…in disagreement with. You see, magic users have lived in hiding for centuries. We don't want non-magic users thinking we are here only for their amusement, or to be used as tools in their wars or daily lives, or worse…we don't want them thinking we are threats to them. They greatly outnumber us, and would easily overpower us if push came to shove. The Arcane Rebellion disagrees with this sentiment. They believe we should overpower the non-magic users and take over the world. They also believe that only certain people should be able to use magic."

"Those three men that you saw at Jefferson High were from the Arcane Rebellion. I think they wanted to recruit the three of you," Mr. Thornfield nodded to Lyra, Elena, and Darian, "into the Arcane Rebellion. I'm not sure where they saw you, or how they knew of you. But we can't rule out the possibility that they are trying to recruit young people, just like us. After all, that's how we've survived for as long as we have."

"Hold on," said Elena sharply. "So you're saying that the Arcane Rebellion is trying to recruit us? Recruit us for what?"

Mr. Thornfield shrugged. "I do not know their plans, for I am not part of them," he said simply. "My role is to find young people and get them to join the Bellwater

Mages. I can say we want you to join us and study magic under our tutelage. But I don't know for sure what the Arcane Rebellion would want of you. The same thing perhaps? Or something completely different. I haven't the faintest idea."

"I see," said Lyra. "So these Arcane Rebellion people…they come to our school, torch the place, and– hold on–what about our families?! Our friends?!"

Mr. Thornfield stared blankly into the pond.

"Mr. Thornfield?! What happened to our families and friends?!"

Mr. Thornfield motioned his hands towards the pond. A large bubble appeared and floated out of the pond towards the sky, but stopped at just the right height for the students to see out of it. It was as though they were watching an outdoor movie on a summer evening.

The students stared into the bubble, and gasped.

Their school–or what remained of it–appeared in the bubble. The school was burned to the ground, thick black smoke rising into the air as firefighters tried to put out the last remnants of the fire. In front of the school was a small group of police officers giving a statement to a local news station:

"At this time, the cause of the fire remains unknown. Arson investigators tell us that foul play is not out of the question, though nothing is confirmed. It is with deep regret that we inform the public that everyone who was in the school, or within a 5-mile radius of the building at the time of the fire—at 3:00 this afternoon—is believed to be dead. We will not be taking questions at this time. Thank you."

The students stared in disbelief at the bubble. It simply floated there for a while as though waiting for the group to change the channel. Then Foxton spoke, and it popped.

"So all our friends...all our families...are—"

"Gone."

Mr. Thornfield stood up. "I'm so sorry for your losses," he said quietly. "If there's anything—"

"There is something you can do!" said Darian quickly. He stood up and looked Mr. Thornfield in the eye. "You could go get them, and you can bring them all back to life just like you did for me."

Mr. Thornfield looked uncomfortable at this suggestion, but it seemed as though he had been expecting it.

"I was going to say," he said firmly, "that if there's anything you need—a fresh change of clothes, some food, a shower—we can get that for you at our cottage, which is not too far from here." Then he said, determinedly not looking at Darian, "I'm sorry, but I cannot do those things for you."

"Why not?!"

"Because that's not how magic works!" snapped Mr. Thornfield. "There are rules to magic. It was incredibly irresponsible for me to bring you back to life when you were dead, and I did it anyway. I very well could have killed myself in the process of bringing you back. But I took a calculated risk, and in my eyes, the payoff for bringing you back was worth the risk to my life. But if I go for all of your friends, then all of your parents, well, we're talking dozens of people being brought back to life. You all saw what bringing Darian back to life did to me. If I do that again to even one more person, that would be about five times worse. Not to mention," he finished, "the police have already announced that all your family and friends are dead. How do you think it will look if they miraculously turn up alive?"

The five students sat in silence at their teacher's words. He was right, of course. There was no debating with him; they had learned, in the three short weeks that they had known Mr. Thornfield, that arguing with him when he was committed to something was a waste of time and energy.

Mr. Thornfield sighed. "I am sorry. Truly. For all of your losses. For now, let's get you to our cottage. It is a short walk, but you will find yourselves much more comfortable there."

He stood up, and it was clear to the group that it was time to go. Foxton sighed, then took one last look around the clearing. He knew he would eventually feel something- sadness, grief, anger - he wasn't sure what, but he knew this feeling of shock and emptiness would eventually subside.

"Mr. Thornfield..?" asked Lyra timidly. "Can I ask you something?"

"Yes, but please!" said Mr. Thornfield kindly, "I really hate being called Mr. Thornfield. Call me Tobias."

Chapter Three:
Bellwater Cottage

"Tobias...where are we?" asked Lyra.

"We are approaching Bellwater Cottage outside the village of Bellwater. We are about five hundred miles away from Jefferson High, give or take."

"And where are we going?" asked Elena.

"We are going to meet my friend, Aurora Wildwood. She is the leader of the Bellwater Mages."

"Is she going to perform some more magic?" asked Darian. He sounded simultaneously anxious and excited about the prospect.

"Probably. Aurora's the strongest, most capable mage I know. She taught me magic when I first started out. She earned her leadership position by killing our last leader."

There was silence at these words, as if the students weren't sure if Tobias was kidding or not. Tobias turned around to look at them.

"I'm not kidding. She disagreed with his view that only certain individuals should study magic. She killed him to get him out of the way so we could teach more students. There is something you should know about her. I love Aurora very much, but she…has something of an anger problem."

"An anger problem?" questioned Foxton incredulously.

"Yes, an anger problem. So don't make her mad, and whatever you do, don't insult her or her branch of magic."

Tobias led his group of students out of the forest clearing and towards a small path that seemed to have been well-traveled. The students, still in a state of shock, followed their ex-teacher with some reluctance, but knew they ultimately had no choice but to do so. Their parents were dead. They could not return home; there was no home for them to return to. They didn't even know where they were.

After walking for a short time, the students started to notice that the path was growing wider, as though they were approaching the edge of the forest.

Just then, a noise came from just ahead on the path.

Tobias frowned.

"Who goes there?!" he called out.

"It is I," announced a strong, female voice.

Out of the clearing walked a tall, beautiful woman with long, brown hair. Quite the opposite of Tobias, she was well dressed and seemed to be one of those people who would hit the gym every day.

"Toby!" she said kindly. "I did not expect you back so soon. You've already found us new students?"

She looked around at the group, and her eyes grew narrow. "You brought five of them at one time, Toby? You've never brought this many at once before." She turned to look at him, then–"What has happened? I can tell something has gone wrong. What is it?"

She sprang away from the group, freeing her hands. She had a certain sense of strength and charisma about her. The students slightly backed away from her, but Tobias simply responded, "We need to talk. Someplace private. Aurora, can we go to Bellwater Cottage?"

Aurora nodded. "Yes, let's go. Follow me!"

She turned and led the way. They went through the rest of the clearing, and the group found themselves on the top of a large hill. Looking down the hill, they saw a small town; there were several houses, and what looked like a few stores, gas stations, a school, and a library. A glance to the other side revealed nothing but a highway and a small cottage overlooking the town.

Aurora led the group toward the cottage. On the outside, the cottage looked small, quaint, and cozy; it was one story tall, with light blue siding, a big front porch, and a garden directly outside. There was a small driveway that had two vehicles to the right of the cottage, but these vehicles looked brand new, as though they didn't really get used often. There was dust starting to collect on them.

The group walked up to the front porch. Aurora

opened the door and gestured to the group to come inside. The inside of the cottage looked exactly like the group would expect. Like a fussy old lady lived there. Aurora closed the door behind them.

"Have a seat, everyone! I'll make us some coffee."

The group sat themselves around a large dining room table while Aurora took out six large mugs and poured coffee that she seemed to have been making for herself. Then she grabbed milk and sugar, put everything on to a large carrying tray, and set the tray on to the table. She also placed a large plate of her homemade brownies on the tray, and Tobias helped himself to one almost at once. The students did the same, accepting the brownie and coffee rather reluctantly.

"I know you don't drink coffee, Tobias. Here," said Aurora, going back to the kitchen, opening the door to the fridge, and tossing a bottle of water at Tobias. "Now, children. What has Tobias told you?"

The students looked around at each other, at the cottage, anywhere but at Aurora. Whoever made eye contact with her would have to answer her questions.

"Lyra, you explain," said Tobias.

"Why don't you just tell her?"

"I want to make sure you understand what I said to you," he replied simply. "And you're the brave one, aren't you? Go ahead; summarize what I told you to Aurora."

Lyra swallowed, then explained to the woman what

had happened. She told her all about how three men had attacked their school with fire, how Tobias had saved them with his magic—she compared him to "a human Pikachu" which made Tobias smile--and brought them to the forest, then explained to them what he did and why he did it.

"So he expects us to join this Bellwater Academy, but we don't really know what it is," she finished.

Aurora took a long sip of her coffee. "I see," she stated after a moment's pause. She put her mug down and then stood up. "Well, let me explain to you who exactly we are.

We are a group of people whose goal is to continue the study of magic without jeopardizing our safety, or the safety of others. We do this by carefully guarding our abilities. The first thing you need to understand—that perhaps was made unclear in your explanation—is that we need to uphold that secret. We do not perform magic out in public, except in extreme circumstances, for fear of being discovered."

Lyra and Elena glanced sideways at each other. "But why don't you just take over? Surely even the military would fall at your hands?"

"Because like I said before," interrupted Tobias, "If we were to do that, or attempt to do that, the non-magic users would overpower us with sheer numbers. Even with all our powers over the elements, there is still greater power in numbers. It is imperative that we keep to ourselves, that we practice in secret. Though, like I said, not all believe that."

Aurora turned to look at Tobias. "You told them of the Arcane Rebellion?" she questioned, sounding surprised and a little angry.

"Of course I did; they were the ones who attacked the school, Aurora. I think Lyra and her friends noticed something was amiss."

Aurora sighed, then her voice cracked with concern as she responded, "I didn't expect this." She took a sip of her coffee.

"So, what happens now?" asked Foxton, who was suspiciously quiet, Tobias thought.

Aurora took a second to gather herself, then said calmly, "We will keep you here for the time being. We have a safe house in town. You will be transferred tomorrow. We don't generally have students stay here, but for tonight, there is no other choice."

"Now, here's the deal."

She went and pointed out the window. There was a clear view of the village down below. "That village is called Bellwater," she said. "Your school–" she pointed towards a building at the very foot of the hill, "is called Bellwater Academy. I will allow you to take the weekend off, but you will be attending starting Monday."

"Please listen carefully to this because it is very important, and I do not wish to repeat myself. You cannot. You can. Not. Tell anyone at Bellwater Academy that you know about magic."

The students blinked at this.

"You will be attending the school with a mixture of students—some of whom are magic users, some of whom are not. Some of your teachers are magic users, and some of them are not. We will not be able to tell you who is who. We expect you to keep the secret."

"And what if we let it slip?" asked Finnian, his voice quivering; he had never been good at keeping secrets.

"We will kill you," said Aurora simply. "And make no mistake; there is no sarcasm there. We have killed students before, and we will do so again. Don't be added to that list. You saw how those guys from the Arcane Rebellion killed your friends, right? It will be a much slower, much more painful death."

The students stared at her, a mixture of fear and apprehension in the air.

"Fear not. We will not harm you so long as you follow this rule. Safety and security are our main priorities."

"Now, a few things to know about the academy."

She stood up and went into the living room for a second, then came back carrying five copies of a small book. The students recognized it as a school planner.

"There is a staff directory in here," she said simply. "You will see I am here as a school counselor. I will be working with you on things like scheduling and career advice. I will be putting together your class schedules and meeting with your teachers to discuss your placements. I will make sure your credits transfer appropriately, and that you are placed in the correct class for your level."

"Wait, is this like Hogwarts or something?" asked Elena excitedly.

"No," said Aurora simply. "Hogwarts doesn't exist. This is an actual high school just like Jefferson High. You will attend this school during the day, and in the evenings, you will go to your safe house and learn magic."

"But what about sports? We play basketball, and we're rather good—" Lyra began.

"No sports," said Aurora firmly. "Your basketball days are done. You will live new lives now as spellcasters."

The twin girls looked sheepishly at each other. Then they asked in unison, "Do we have to?"

Aurora stared at them, surprised. "You don't want to learn magic?"

"We want to keep playing basketball," said Lyra. "If we have to pick between that or magic, we choose basketball."

"Sweetheart, why do you care so much about basketball?" asked Aurora gently. "There's no future in it for you. We both know you will play through high school, maybe college, if you're lucky. We don't want you to peak so young in life. Think about your future!"

Lyra looked as though she had been slapped in the face.

"Now, I need to reiterate to all of you the importance of keeping magic our little secret. What do you do if someone asks you if you're aware that there's a rumor going around that magic exists?"

The students stared around at each other, not knowing what to say to this. "You laugh and say that's ridiculous," offered Tobias.

"Yes, thank you, Tobias!" exclaimed Aurora, who seemed to be losing patience. "Yes, you laugh it off. Make a joke about it. Or just play dumb. I don't care who asks you. I don't care how they ask you. The word 'magic' is a curse word for all I care. I don't expect to hear any of you talking about it. Understood?"

"Understood," the group repeated.

"Good. Now, let me bring the five of you upstairs. I'll show you where you'll be sleeping."

Aurora led the group of students up the stairs. "Oh, and Tobias," she called. "Stay and visit for a while, won't you?"

Tobias, who had no intentions of going anywhere, helped himself to another brownie. After about fifteen minutes, Aurora came downstairs.

"They're still in shock, Tobias," she said. "We'll have to keep an eye on them."

"Yes, we will—hold on. We?"

"Yes, we," said Aurora. "You don't think I'm going to send you back out there so soon?"

"Why wouldn't you?"

"I don't know, Tobias. Maybe because you just got attacked by the Arcane Rebellion?"

"Oh, come now, Aurora! It was a coincidence. They were after those kids—"

"Oh really? They were after five kids who didn't even know about magic until they attacked? You don't think it was more likely they were after you?"

Tobias hadn't really considered that possibility. "Hunter was one of them," he said sheepishly. Then he thought about it a bit more. "He didn't realize I'd be there, though. He was surprised to see me."

Aurora blinked. "I see," she said. "This changes things. They were almost definitely after the kids, then."

She sat down and helped herself to more coffee and one of her brownies. Aurora wasn't much of a cook, but she did make a great brownie; really, any kind of baking was Aurora's specialty.

"I think you need to lay low for a while," she said after a few minutes. "Stay here."

"You want me to stay in the cottage? And what, sit around and watch television all day?"

"Well...no."

"So, what?"

"I want you to come to the school and substitute teach for a while," she said slowly. But then she sighed. "But Percival has been a big pain in my butt the last few weeks."

Percival Ion was the principal of Bellwater Academy. He was, notably, not a magic user. He was also stubborn, and had a reputation for being unfair, unjust, and just plain rude.

"I don't want to work for him, Aurora. How you've managed to do so for so long–"

"It's been easy," she said. "But something has changed in the last few months. It seems like he's...not on to us per se, but he's not giving me as much leeway as he used to."

Tobias frowned. Despite Percival's reputation, he had also historically been open to letting Aurora just do whatever she wanted.

"Have the others noticed?"

"Some of them have, yes," she said. "Ion's been cracking down on a lot of us. Not giving us as much flexibility, or freedom. Starting to kind of micromanage us."

"Sounds like every other public high school in the nation."

Aurora smiled at him. "Still not enjoying your

assignment then, Toby?"

"No, not especially. Behavior problems galore at virtually every school, and I can hardly even teach. Administrators micromanaging our every move. Parents thinking their crotch goblins can do no wrong. Politicians thinking teachers are to blame for the failed educational system—"

"Yes, I've heard this speech a thousand times, Toby. Why haven't you asked what else you could be doing to help us?"

"Because I've no other talents."

"Nonsense!"

"Well, what else can I do to help, Aurora?"

She blinked, then quickly said, "I'll have to give it some thought, Tobias. But I hate seeing you so miserable."

Tobias sighed. "See, even you don't know what else I could be doing to help."

They both laughed. This was the kind of friendship they had; they knew each other well enough to support and pick on each other.

"Alright, well, thank you for your help, Aurora. I'm going to call it a night."

Tobias stood up. He walked towards the door of the cottage.

"Where are you going?" asked Aurora.

"I just feel like being alone for a while," he said simply.

"Well…okay. But if you get lonely or want company, you come back here. Oh, and I almost forgot to tell you— Percival did hire a new teacher that I think you should meet."

Tobias turned to look at Aurora, raising his eyebrows.

"Oh? Why's that?"

"I think you'd like him. And you could use a friend like him."

"Nonsense, Aurora! You're the only friend I need."

Chapter Four:
Perfect Moments

Tobias left the small cottage. He needed some time alone. It had been a long day; he was feeling sick of people after the events that took place at Jefferson High, and then the events that took place in the clearing within the forest.

He was thinking of Darian. He had never actually brought anyone back to life before with his magic, although he had seen it done once. Reviving Darian from death was something he didn't regret doing per se, but he did feel rather tired, weak, and ready to isolate for a while.

Tobias would never consider himself to be a lonely person; he preferred to think of himself as "Mister Independent" - not needing anyone or anything else to survive a world he considered to be cold, cruel, and calculating. He had been hurt too many times in the past by people he believed to be friends to really have much of a need for them. He did this thing where he essentially became a hermit, avoiding all human interaction for a period of time, until his energy returned, and he was ready to face the world again.

I just need a minute, he thought to himself as he walked. *That's all I need. Just a minute to myself.*

These "minutes" turned more into hours, then entire

days, then weekends and, on one occasion, a full week where he was alone. He didn't talk to anyone. He didn't reach out to anyone, nor did anyone attempt to contact him. With his teaching positions, this tended to happen most often in the summertime. He needed that time to reset and recharge from the previous school year in preparation for the next one.

This time around was different. It was only September. He shouldn't need this. He had just had the entire summer off to rest and recharge. He should have accepted Aurora's invitation to stay in her place for the evening and get some rest there.

But he couldn't. He needed some alone time.

As he walked, the events from earlier in the day continued to weigh heavily on his mind. He also pondered several questions. The thing that was weighing the most heavily on his mind was Hunter.

Tobias and Hunter had a…complicated history. They were best friends in high school and had been recruited by none other than Aurora herself while they were in high school. Their circumstances could not have been more different than the students whom Tobias had just brought to Bellwater. Aurora had waited until their junior year to invite them to Bellwater Academy, where she promised to teach them the power of the elements. Tobias had jumped at this possibility. Hunter had jumped at the prospect of getting to spend two years with Tobias. Neither of them had any parents or families to worry about either; as far as Tobias knew, all of their families were dead.

Tobias smiled as he called to mind a specific memory he had had with Hunter.

They were sitting next to each other, having a laugh, when three large men came over and asked them what they were doing. Things soon turned ugly as the men decided they didn't like the implications of Tobias and Hunter enjoying an evening down by the river, alone, together.

Luckily, Tobias had a much clearer head than Hunter, who had been drinking. In his drunken stupor, he actually started to launch a fire attack on one of the men who was walking, fists clenched, in his direction. But Tobias stopped him and used magic to teleport the two of them away from the scene.

"Why'd you stop me? I could've taken them!"

"Yes, Hunter, you could've. And you would've killed them. Then we'd have to deal with the police and campus security, not to mention the military and whoever else they'd send for us. Please, let's just drop it. Okay?"

Hunter was not the type of person to just let something like that go. Tobias knew that it had continued to haunt him, every day. Hunter took a lot of pride in being what he would consider a protector of Tobias. The two hardly ever left each other's sights throughout their college years; they had the same classes, and the same work schedules. They were roommates. At one point, they were very nearly something more. Tobias loved how Hunter would've done anything to protect him. It made him feel special, wanted.

His thoughts then went to his last meeting with Hunter.

Hunter used to be one of his colleagues, and filled a very similar role to that of Tobias himself: recruiting possible new students for Bellwater Academy to help train them into spellcasters. Like Tobias, Hunter had chosen to target high school students specifically for this mission. But unlike Tobias, Hunter had been rather unsuccessful at it.

Hunter had what some would consider to be very poor classroom management skills. He had allowed the students to walk all over him; he considered himself to be the students' friend, and he did not have consequences for poor choices within his classroom. This led to Hunter losing more than one teaching job in the past. Last Tobias had heard, Hunter was searching for teaching employment and refused to come back to Bellwater until he had found something. Tobias had no idea he had joined the Arcane Rebellion until a few hours ago. He had no idea what Hunter had been up to over the last year, despite his best efforts to keep tabs on his former friend.

Tobias sighed as he arrived back at the clearing in the forest. Those moments, those perfect moments with Hunter, were just that…moments. And even perfect moments couldn't be held on to forever. The clock would eventually tick, the moment would end, and life would move on.

His mind went to the last time he had seen Hunter, a year ago, they were discussing how Hunter believed they should be a little less selective about who should be allowed at Bellwater Academy:

"We need recruits, Toby! We need as many as we can get. We're trying to ensure that magic continues on, right?

Well, the more people, the better! Quantity over quality, in this case, I say!"

But Tobias disagreed.

"No, Hunt! It's not that simple. Not just anyone can perform magic. It's just like any other skill: it takes lots of practice, concentration, and devotion. Plus, you need to have emotion, and people need to love you. Not sure how you ever got that part down!"

Tobias smiled, then wiped a single tear out of his eye. He really did miss Hunter. Unfortunately, he rather doubted that the feeling was reciprocated. That disagreement had been much bigger than he had realized; going after Hunter's lack of emotion had touched something of a nerve for him. For he had lashed out and stricken Tobias with a ball of flames.

"What the hell, man? What was that for?!"

They had started to fight. Fire and lightning clashed in midair, Hunter wielded fire, Tobias controlled lightning and wind.

They had been right here, in this clearing, when it had happened. He had never seen Hunter lose control like this, especially over something as trivial as a disagreement about who should be allowed to attend Bellwater Academy.

The forest around them was slowly destroyed. Hunter threw fireball after fireball at Tobias, who blocked them with lightning. Tobias had directed his magic towards the pond; the water in the pond leapt up and surrounded Hunter, then immobilized him. But Hunter used his firepower and evaporated all of the pond's water almost instantly.

Tobias reached for the skies and pointed at a nearby cloud; the cloud shot a bolt of lightning down on Hunter. It hit him square in the back of the head; Hunter screamed and lit the nearby treetops on fire.

"Enough!"

Aurora stepped in, seemingly from out of nowhere. She used her own magic to put out Hunter's fire on the treetops; the trees instantly restored themselves. Aurora was the reason this clearing always looked pristine; her magic allowed it to constantly regrow and remedy itself.

When someone chooses to study magic, they first choose a type of magic to specialize in, though it is possible to have more than one if you desired. Tobias chose to specialize in water, wind, and lightning magic. Sure, it meant he was a little weaker in each one, but he had a greater variety in his toolbox. Hunter, on the other hand, had chosen to focus exclusively on fire magic; therefore, he was much stronger in that one area but had no variety in his spells.

Aurora was a master of earth magic. There was a reason she enjoyed gardening as much as she did; she had a perfect green thumb. She didn't even need fertile soil or anything. Just a little bit of magic would turn a seed into a fully bloomed plant. On the surface level, magic users would underestimate her and her love of the earth, but

Aurora's earthquakes would quickly squash anything resembling contempt for her magic. However, she also had a particular penchant for frost, which is how she put out the fire on the treetops; a quick frost over the tops had put it out as quickly as Hunter had started it.

Tobias was so caught up in his thoughts that he failed to register that there was someone else in the clearing with him. He had just spent the better part of an hour reminiscing about Hunter, and missing him terribly that to hear a voice made him jump:

"What are you doing here?"

He didn't recognize the voice. Confused, Tobias looked around.

"Who's there?"

"I'm right here."

It was a young man standing next to the tree where Tobias had been ill earlier. It was hard to make out his features in the darkness.

"How long have you been here?"

"A little while. Needed some time to myself. I just noticed you, in fact. Been kinda lost in thought…"

"Yeah, me too…"

The two men stared at each other for a little bit. Then

Tobias asked, "I'm sorry, but who are you?"

The man grinned. "I'm Odion. Odion Montgomery. Who are you?"

"Tobias. Tobias Thornfield. What are you doing here, Odion?"

"I'm new in town. Just started teaching at the school. Went exploring one day and found this little clearing. Been coming up almost every night since."

"Really?"

"Yes. Are you new in town as well?"

"Not exactly. Just been out of town for a while. Back now, visiting."

"I see. Well, I'll leave you to it, Tobias. It was nice to meet you."

Odion smiled at Tobias, then walked away down the path where Tobias had led the students mere hours ago. Tobias frowned.

Only magic-users should know about this spot, he thought to himself. But I can't trust him to be just a regular guy who stumbled upon this clearing.

He shook his head, then decided to get some sleep. He pulled up a nearby rock and found his supply of blankets and pillows underneath. He liked to keep to himself, and found he frequented this spot often enough he kept a small supply of pillows and blankets under his favorite rock in the clearing for occasions such as this. He made a nice little bed for himself by the pond, then used magic to cast some basic protection around the clearing, as well as give him some warmth. Especially after Odion, he wanted to be careful not to let his guard down too much. Soon enough, Tobias found himself drifting off to sleep.

Chapter Five:
Confronting Shadows

Tobias awoke late the next morning. After the events of the previous day, he had had trouble staying asleep; he couldn't get the images of those poor girls, and his former colleagues, burning alive, dying right in front of him.

Hunter was the cause of all of this, no less. Hunter…

He sat up. He knew what he had to do. But it would be risky; Aurora would be displeased if he went without telling her what he planned to do. He checked his watch; it was 11am. Aurora would be awake, it was Saturday, but he knew she was busy dealing with the students. He didn't really want to see them; he felt it was best if he simply left them alone for at least today.

Tobias spent most of the afternoon lounging around the clearing. He didn't eat; he rarely ate anything. He just didn't feel like it. It would be a lot of work to go into town and pick something up, though he was somewhat tempted by the idea of a greasy cheeseburger that the local bar made better than anywhere else he had ever been. But it was too much fuss for him; he just wanted to be alone with his thoughts for a while. Aurora would fix him something when he got to her house; he was sure of it.

He thought about Hunter, what he was doing, how he

could live with himself for working so closely with the Arcane Rebellion. He wondered what their plans were, where he was at.

But I could try to look, he thought to himself. He had done it just yesterday; he used his magic to examine the situation with his former employer. Scrying was something virtually any magic user could do.

But it was a long shot that it would work; spellcasters could easily prevent others from scrying on them. And it was risky; even if it worked, Hunter would probably notice that someone was trying to scry on him, and it was even likely that Hunter would realize it was Tobias. Tobias wasn't exactly scared of Hunter, but he still didn't like the idea of the Arcane Rebellion raining down on him if Hunter decided to gather some of his friends to ransack the place.

Instead, his thoughts wandered to that of Foxton, Finnian, Elena, Lyra, and Darian. How they were adjusting. He thought Aurora rushing them into this new school system was perhaps a bit misguided, that perhaps she should have allowed them to lay low for a few weeks to digest what had happened to their homes and their families. But he also saw it from the perspective that keeping the students busy was better for them in the long run than allowing them to dwell on things they could not change. They would need counseling for sure, though Tobias supposed Aurora would know that as the guidance counselor.

Finally, it was five o'clock in the evening. He figured Aurora would be back at her cottage by now. He didn't bother walking; he simply teleported himself back to the front door of her cottage. It was generally frowned upon to teleport directly into someone's home; people didn't tend to like it when you appeared seemingly out of nowhere directly inside their living room. Not to mention, Aurora had cast spells around her place to prevent such a thing from occurring.

He knocked on the front door. Aurora answered it.

"Toby!"

They hugged. It wasn't entirely unusual for them to hug, but it normally came after long, deep talks about their emotions and happenings. It was extremely unusual for her to hug him out of nowhere.

"I have company. I think you'll like him!"

She whispered that into his ear, and he instantly turned to leave, but she grabbed his arm. "No, no, no, Tobias! You're not going anywhere."

"Tobias?"

He turned to look at the new arrival. It was Odion Montgomery, the man he had met at the clearing last night. Tobias was taken aback at the appearance of Odion, a handsome young man, his attractive features much more prominent in the daylight than they had been in the darkness of the night. He had short, black hair that was well-groomed. His build was that of an off-season athlete, as though he was training to keep himself in shape. Like Aurora, it was obvious this was a man who took good care of himself.

"Hello, Odyeon, was it?"

"Er...it's Odion. Pronounced Ode-ee-on."

Tobias grimaced. "Sorry. Odion. Nice to officially meet you."

Tobias extended a hand, and Odion shook it.

"You two know each other?" asked Aurora.

"Yes, we met last night," said Odion.

Aurora turned to look at him. "You went out to the clearing?"

"Yes, I discovered it my first week here, before school started."

"I see. That is Tobias' favorite spot. You might have to fight him for it."

Odion smiled. His smile was warm and friendly, his white teeth glimmered. "No need for that. If it's a problem, I'll leave that spot alone and find another one."

"No!" said Tobias quickly. Too quickly, he soon realized. Aurora and Odion looked at him. "Er–that's to say, you don't need to find another spot. Plenty of room for both of us, eh?"

Aurora looked at Tobias, a little twinkle in her eye. Tobias hated it when she looked at him that way, like she knew his deepest, darkest secrets. Odion just smiled at Tobias.

"Well, thank you, Tobias! That's very kind of you."

"Odion is a teacher at the school with me, Tobias," said Aurora simply. "And speaking of the school, I have a new task for you."

"What is it?"

"I'd like you to apply to be a substitute. One of our teachers is out for a while; she fell and may have broken her hip. Why Agatha refuses to retire is beyond me–"

"No," said Tobias firmly. "I am not substituting for Agatha O'Connor."

Agatha O'Connor was the oldest teacher at Bellwater Academy. The English and literature teacher, she had a reputation for being fair, but strict. She had never seemed to like Tobias much; he suspected she thought he was lazy. Aurora's comment about her refusing to retire, however, was spot on; she was one of those people who lived to work, not worked to live. She also did, however, happen to be a spellcaster; she had a particular affinity for water magic, though she dabbled in lightning magic from time to time. She would often try to coach Tobias on how he performed his magic, though Tobias took great enjoyment in the fact that he was a far superior magician to Agatha O'Connor. Granted, her old age undoubtedly had something to do with that, but he paid that trivial fact no mind.

"Tobias, come on–"

"No, Aurora. You know what's going to happen. Percival Ion seems to think no one can hold a candle to Agatha's teaching methods. He'll sit there and compare me to her the whole time I'm teaching for her. And if she broke her hip, she'd be out for several weeks. I can't take that kind of pressure for several weeks, Aurora!"

"No one said you need to do it for several weeks," said Aurora calmly. Her calmness did help to bring Tobias down a level. "Just do it for a couple of days. We really need someone, and I want to make sure it's someone I can trust. Just give Percival a call, okay?"

"I can put in a good word for you, too," chimed Odion. "Percival and I have a good relationship."

"No thanks," Tobias replied coldy. "I can do this on my own, you know."

"I didn't say you couldn't," Odion retorted, shrugging. "I just figured I'd offer. No need to bite my head off."

Tobias took a deep breath. "No, you're right. Thank you for the offer. Percival and I have a history. I've subbed there before. And we know how that's gone, don't we, Aurora?"

Aurora smiled. "Yes, but this time, you have me backing you up. I'm not just a lowly teacher anymore, Tobias. I'm the guidance counselor. I already told Percival you'd be down to do it. He expects you at eight o'clock

Monday morning."

Tobias sighed. Leave it to Aurora to make plans for him without consulting him first.

"Actually, Aurora. There's something I need to do."

Aurora looked at him, suspicious. Tobias took a deep breath.

"I need to talk to Hunter."

Aurora held up a hand to silence him; he obeyed at once. Aurora turned to Odion.

"Odion, I'm terribly sorry. Would you excuse us for a moment?"

"Oh, no worries, Aurora," said Odion politely. "I need to be going anyway; it's getting late, and I certainly don't want to intrude on your dinner. Thank you again for the consultation!"

He stood up, walked to the door, and opened it. "Oh, and Tobias, it was really nice to see you again." He smiled at Tobias, then left without another word.

Aurora turned to face Tobias. "No, Tobias!" she shrieked. He was expecting this kind of reaction. "You are not going to go and talk to him!"

"Aurora, please! I need to find out why–"

"Why did he join the Arcane Rebellion? I don't see how it's any of your business to know, Tobias! The fact is, he joined, and he burned bridges with us the moment he did!"

"I see what you did there. Burned. Cause, you know, fire magic…"

"Shut up, Tobias! This is no time for your stupid jokes!"

"Aurora, calm down!" Barked Tobias. "Look! My asking is a formality. I'm going to find him whether you want me to or not."

Aurora took a deep breath. Then she took another. Then she took several more. Finally, after a few minutes, she said quietly, "And how exactly do you plan to take on the entire Arcane Rebellion single-handedly? I cannot be there with you, Tobias!"

"I don't plan to take them on. I'll be stealthy. I just want to make sure he's okay, Aurora—"

"He hurt you, Tobias! He broke your heart. He crushed you. He broke you, and I was left to pick up the pieces. If you do this—if he breaks you again—" she wiped a tear away from her eye—"I can't—I can't pick up the pieces again, Toby. I can't do it."

Tobias stood, watching Aurora. He had never seen her lose control like this. Never. It was common for her to get angry, but to get so emotional and to *cry* about it was very much unlike her.

They stood in silence for what felt like hours, neither of them saying anything. It seemed as though neither wanted to be the one to break the silence. Finally, Aurora said, "Are you hungry? I should eat something."

Tobias frowned at her. "No, not really. Actually, I should go—"

"No, Tobias. We are finishing what we started."

Aurora looked back at him, her face sad, but determined. "If this is what you want to do, then I cannot stop you. But I also can't let you go alone. I want you to bring someone. For backup and support."

"Who? Agatha broke her hip. You're too busy; you said it yourself. Who else could—"

"Odion."

Tobias blinked. "Is he—is he a spellcaster?"

"He's learning. I want you to teach him."

"He's brand new, Aurora. You've known him for, what, three weeks?"

"Four, actually. Met him during in-service. And you're one to talk. You've known those kids you brought here, what, three weeks? You don't know them nearly as well as I know Odion."

"Yeah, but what are the kids gonna do? They're just kids, Aurora. But a spellcaster—"

"A novice spellcaster who will be fulfilling a task with one of our strongest spellcasters, and learning from him in the process."

"Why can't one of the others—Sabrina or Lucien or Matilda—"

"We can't spare any other teachers, Toby."

"You'd need a sub for Odion. Plus, it's a replacement for Agatha when she's out. What's the difference—"

"The difference between losing a first-year teacher and a senior teacher is night and day, as you know, Toby. The others can sub for Odion as needed. I have another sub lined up to take over for Agatha in a couple of days."

Aurora turned away from him. "Oh, but this isn't to happen until the end of next week. I told Percival you'd be in this week for Agatha; you are not making me out to be a liar."

Tobias sighed. He figured that was about as good as he was going to get.

"Now, you're staying, and you're eating. What have you eaten today?"

"Nothing."

"Toby. We talked about this."

"I didn't feel like it." He was sulking, he knew it. He also knew Aurora hated it. But he didn't care.

"Well, you're eating," she said. She turned the stove on and started taking knives, cutting boards, and pots and pans out of cupboards. "Come here, make yourself useful! Grab the potatoes and start peeling them."

Chapter Six:
Substitute Teaching

Tobias awoke early Monday morning. He had spent the previous day hanging around the cottage and spending time with Aurora. He was in Aurora's guest bedroom; he remembered the wonderful day they shared together. He hadn't seen her in what felt like a long time, though it had only been a few weeks.

He got out of bed and took a shower. This was a special occasion for him; Tobias typically only showered once or twice a week, but after the events of the last few days, he felt he could use one. After his shower, he returned to the spare bedroom, where he wandered to the closet. He put on a button-down shirt and tie with some dress slacks (Percival Ion would comment on his attire if he wore anything less). He really did look miles better now than he had at Jefferson, even before the fire. After getting ready, he walked downstairs, where he found Aurora making breakfast.

"Ah, good morning, Toby!"

"Good morning, Aurora."

"You look lovely this morning. I'm glad to see you dressed up!"

"Yes, well, if I didn't, we both know Percival would say something. And I'm not in the mood to deal with him today."

Aurora pursed her lips but didn't say anything in response to this. The reality was, he was right, and she knew it; Tobias and Percival didn't always see eye to eye.

They ate breakfast in a comfortable silence, like an old married couple. The truth was, Tobias and Aurora had always been like this: comfortable being around each other, though no romantic interaction had ever taken place. When they were out in public, they often got mistaken for being boyfriend/girlfriend or even husband/wife, though that couldn't be further from the truth. They were best friends. Aurora had saved Toby's life on more than one occasion, and Toby had saved Aurora, too. Though he didn't realize it, she needed him just as much as he needed her. She had been a young teacher—early 20's—when she recruited Tobias and Hunter to the Bellwater Mages, so their age difference was only about four or five years.

They drove to school together. It was imperative, Aurora had said, to keep up appearances; they could easily teleport to the school, probably directly into Aurora's office, and no one would ever know. But it would be too suspicious if they were seen just appearing out of nowhere and someone like Percival Ion happened to see them.

The magic of teleportation was indeed a useful tool, but it had its limitations. First, distance did matter; no spellcaster could realistically teleport more than maybe two thousand miles away from their current location. Shorter distances would not require much effort, but longer distances would take a considerable amount of energy to traverse. Second, if someone were to try teleporting to a location they have never been to previously, there was a high likelihood they would miss their mark and end up in the complete opposite direction of where they were intending to go. Third, it was nearly impossible to guarantee that the spellcaster would not be discovered; on more than one instance, Tobias had teleported to a location and found, to his dismay, that there were already people located there. There was one instance in his first year of teaching where he had teleported directly into his classroom to see that he had forgotten to close the curtains the day before. In that instance, he had found himself staring at a student looking through the window of the classroom. That student swore up and down that "Mr. Thornfield just appeared out of thin air! I swear!" Of course, no one had believed him, but the incident had left Tobias more aware of how careful he needed to be regarding teleportation.

With that knowledge, Tobias and Aurora set out in her car. It was not a long drive, about five minutes in total. They parked, and Tobias looked at the school as they started to walk in.

The school was a small, relatively run-down building. It had only one level. Windows lined up and down the side of the building; it looked like one window per classroom. Approximately half of the windows had small cracks in them. The front doors leading into the building looked rather unimpressive; a faded, old-fashioned cartoon mascot had been painted on the front door of the school. Right above the front doors was a sign that creaked in the wind, reading "Bellwater Academy." Tobias knew the building was old; it had been built over one hundred years prior and had only ever had one upgrade (the state had made a surprise visit and told them they needed to remove some steps leading into the school to make it ADA- compliant). This upgrade consisted of basically removing the steps and calling it good. Any parent looking at the school would think twice about sending their child to a school with a building that looked as run down as this was.

The school only served students in grades nine through twelve. The elementary and middle school, both housed in much newer buildings, were on the other side of town. Most of those students would go on to do high school mostly online or attend the high school that was about twenty miles out of town with a brand-new building and several more opportunities in sports and the arts.

Tobias' group of magic users picked this school for this reason: the fewer non-magic users who were part of this school community, the better. Unfortunately, there were so few magic users that it would be impractical to try to have a school of their own. It was better, much better, to blend in at an existing school than to try and start one up on their own.

Tobias and Aurora entered the building. To the right was the office. Aurora opened the door and held it open for Tobias. He entered, looking around.

The office was small and cluttered, not the most welcoming of places. A small window overlooked the school parking lot and the town to the right of Tobias. To the left was the nurse's station. The school hadn't actually had a nurse in several years; it was left up to the individual teachers to give their students things like Band-Aids and Tums. Anything more serious than that was up to the school secretary, a short and squat woman in her late 50s who was wearing a frilly purple cardigan and sitting at a small desk in the center of the room. The secretary's name was Beatrice Mistweaver.

Beatrice looked up at the arrival of Aurora and Tobias.

"Good morning, Ms. Wildwood!" She said, nodding at Aurora. "Oh, and Mr. Thornfield. You're back. How…delightful."

It could not have been more obvious that she was being sarcastic.

"Beatrice," said Tobias contemptuously. "I am here for my substitute assignment."

"Of course, Tobias," replied Beatrice. "Here's the folder. Good luck!"

She gave the folder to Tobias. He took it from her and opened it. There were several pages of detailed lesson plans, seating charts, and notes on each of the students. Tobias chuckled.

"Leave it to Agatha to leave me a novel."

"You're in room 18," said Beatrice. "I assume you remember how to get there?"

Tobias nodded, then turned around and exited the office. Aurora bid him a good day and went to her own office across the hall. Tobias began walking down the hallway towards room 18.

Lockers lined the sides of the hallway. They were old and run down; the students didn't generally use them for much anymore, and they were really more of an eyesore than anything else at this point. The school didn't even provide locks, and despite safety concerns, there was never a ban on students carrying backpacks around with them to all their classes. So that's what they did; each student was carrying a solid thirty pounds of weight on their backs to and from each of their classes, about six hours a day.

Leave it to the public school system to give students back problems before they even turn 18, thought Tobias to himself. The more time he invested in the public education system, the more he loathed it.

"Tobias!"

Tobias looked up. There was a tall, slender man standing in front of him, wearing a button-down shirt and tie with black dress pants. This man was Percival Ion, the school principal. He was younger than he looked; he had pale gray hair, and his face was lined with wrinkles. He wore glasses that made his eyes look magnified about ten times their normal size. The man was no older than forty- five, but if Tobias didn't know better, he would've guessed he was sixty-five and close to retirement.

"Mr. Ion."

"You're here for Agatha today, aren't you?" "Yes, sir."

"Do try to maintain the high standards she has set for her students, won't you?"

"What do you mean, sir?"

"Well...it's just that Agatha consistently holds her students to the highest standard. She has the most engaging lesson plans of any teacher here. She builds relationships and lets the students know she cares, getting the most buy-in from students and parents in her classes. She does it all. I expect this from all of my teachers, Tobias. Some of them are on the right track. But no one does it like Agatha."

Yes, thought Tobias. And if you knew how much this job was killing Agatha, you'd be hating yourself for saying all of these things to me.

Tobias smiled and nodded. "It is an honor to serve her classroom and your school, sir," he said. He knew he sounded fake, and he knew his smile was more of a grimace, but he tried.

Percival wasn't fooled. "You are no Agatha, Tobias. Just do your best. Even you can't screw up one day of substitute teaching."

He walked away, back in the direction of the main office. Tobias instantly dropped his smile and walked the rest of the way to classroom 18. It was at the far end of the hallway; he knew that Agatha's classroom was the largest classroom in the whole school. Being the world's greatest teacher in the eyes of the principal certainly had its perks.

He unlocked the classroom with the key from the folder Beatrice had given him and entered the room. The room was large and made to look even larger by the strand of lights hanging from the walls. There were thirty desks facing the front of the room. The teacher's desk was in the front left corner. The room looked tidy, pristine, and ready to go for the day. Tobias went and sat down at the teacher's desk and reviewed the plans for the day.

The day looked pretty straightforward. The first hour was ninth-grade English. They would be reading the book *To Kill a Mockingbird* and completing a short quiz on their reading. The second hour was eleventh-grade English, who would be reenacting the play *Romeo & Juliet*. That would be an interesting hour. The third hour was a prep hour: no class. The fourth hour was senior English, who would be reading *Animal Farm* and, like the ninth grade, completing a short quiz on the reading. Then it was lunchtime. The afternoon classes looked just as busy. The fifth hour was tenth-grade composition, who would be taking a test. The sixth hour was a study hall. Then, the seventh hour was an elective course in public speaking. They were to be practicing their speeches today. All in all, it seemed like a busy but enjoyable day.

Tobias heard someone enter the classroom. He looked up and saw a tall, beautiful woman. He recognized her; she had long, wavy blonde hair and glasses. She was wearing a red dress with red high heels and deep red lipstick. She had red eye shadow and was wearing a strong perfume that smelled of roses.

"Good morning, Sabrina," said Tobias politely. "To what do I owe the pleasure?"

Sabrina Braithwaite was the Science teacher with the classroom across the hall from Agatha O'Connor. Sabrina was also a magic user, Tobias knew. But they were forbidden by Aurora to discuss magic within the halls of Bellwater Academy, for safety and privacy reasons. Sabrina and Tobias knew each other, but he wouldn't exactly call them close.

"Good morning, Tobias," said Sabrina, smiling widely at him. "I just wanted to greet you."

Tobias smiled at her. "It'll be good to be hallmates, Sabrina."

"How long has it been since you were here?"

"About…twelve years since I've been here as a student. I subbed here on and off a few years ago, but I accepted a few other teaching positions since I've been here."

"So, what brings you back?"

Tobias found this something of an odd question. Surely, Aurora would have told her, and the other members, what had happened. He looked at her with a puzzled look, then she added, "Oh, I just meant what brings you back to Bellwater Academy, specifically." She winked at him, still smiling.

"Ah. Agatha needed a substitute teacher. She fell and broke her hip, it seems."

Sabrina gasped and covered her mouth with her hand.

"She fell and broke her hip?! At her age? That's terrible!"

"I know," said Tobias grimly. "So, I'm glad she's taking a few weeks off to rest and recover."

"Yes, goodness knows she deserves it! Well, have a good day, Tobias. Let me know if you need anything."

She waved at him, then left the classroom.

The bell rang five minutes later. The freshmen students filed into the room, not quietly. There was lots of pushing and shoving happening as they entered the classroom. Tobias started his day by yelling at the group-generally not his favorite way to start the day. Halfway through the hour, one of the boys got up and punched another boy in the face seemingly out of nowhere. Tobias yelled at him to stop, but the boy ignored him; fists flew between the two boys, and eventually, the boys collapsed in a heap in the middle of the classroom floor. Tobias had called the office for help, and Beatrice had to come in and separate the boys, then escort them back to the office. Tobias cleaned up the blood that had spilled in between the first and second periods.

The second hour started out fine enough, but the girl who was playing Juliet ended up telling Romeo, in front of the whole class as part of her monologue, that she was going to cut off his penis and perform sexual acts on him with his own penis. Tobias asked her to leave, and she spent the next ten minutes arguing with him about how she was simply expressing herself and acting in the moment. Lyra, Elena, and Darian were in this class; they did not speak to Tobias nor make any indication that they knew who he was. Tobias was slightly hurt by this; he had, after all, quite literally saved their lives two days prior. But he shook it off. If the students didn't want to say hello to him, who was he to force them to? And he supposed it would be strange for the new kids to know the sub already.

The third hour could not have come quickly enough. Tobias spent time reviewing the rest of the plans for the day, and left notes for Agatha on the behavior of the first two classes.

About halfway through the hour, a woman wearing thick glasses entered the classroom. She had curly brown hair and was dressed in jeans and a cardigan. Tobias recognized her at once: Matilda Carrington, the Special Education teacher. Like Sabrina, he knew her, though not well.

"Good morning, Matilda," said Tobias politely. "I'm on my prep now. Was there something you needed?"

"Oh, sorry, er–"

"Tobias." It had been a while since their last meeting, though Tobias was slightly disappointed that she didn't even remember his name.

"Oh, yes. Tobias. I didn't know you were subbing for Agatha."

Matilda was also a member of the Bellwater Mages,

though she was relatively low-ranking. Her role was mostly to facilitate the training of the new apprentices.

"Yes, I am. How are the five new students doing so far? Foxton, Finnian, Lyra, Elena, and Darian?"

"Oh, they're still in shock. Haven't really had much of a chance to work with them, if I'm being honest. I've been busy with the last–"

"Matilda," said Tobias warningly. "I meant, how are they doing here, at Bellwater Academy?"

"Oh!" Matilda looked shocked at her mistake: they weren't supposed to discuss magic at the school. "Well, I haven't met them yet, truth be told."

"I see. Did you need something from me or Agatha?" "I

had a question for Agatha."

"Perhaps I could answer it?"

"I don't think so. It's about a student. Not one you would know–not one of the new students."

"Ah, I see. Well, I'm sure there's another teacher you could ask."

"Yes…I'll go ask Sabrina during her prep hour. Sorry to bother you, Tobias."

She turned and left the room, looking as though she had another place to be. Tobias sighed and continued to leave his notes for Agatha. Special Education had its own challenges and rewards, that was for damn sure.

The fourth hour was the seniors, and Tobias was greeted by Foxton and Finnian enthusiastically at the start of the hour. By far, Tobias's most enjoyable class of the day, he had a great lesson teaching students how Animal Farm continued to be relevant in today's society. He shared with the students that in his opinion, humankind was being overworked just like the horse and needed to take a stand against the politicians and the corporate business people hoarding all of the country's wealth. He left that class with a big smile on his face. But the thing that made him smile most was how Finnian had been so talkative and receptive to him; this was quite unusual from the shy boy that Tobias had known previously.

After the fourth hour, Tobias went into the teacher's lounge for lunch. He found it occupied by Aurora, Sabrina, and a man Tobias recognized as Lucien Rodson, the Art and Music teacher. Bellwater Academy didn't have funding to have two teachers for these "extracurricular" classes, even though they were among the most important subjects taught in Tobias's opinion. Another failure of the public education system, if you asked him. Cut the subjects that matter.

Aurora looked up at him when he entered the teacher's lounge. Tobias didn't bring a lunch of his own and had planned on not eating, but Aurora pulled an extra sandwich out of her lunchbox and handed it to Tobias, smiling widely at him.

"How's the day going so far, Toby?"

"About as expected. Broke up a fight. Had a girl make threats against a young man's privates. Had a visit from Matilda. Had a great lesson last hour, though."

"Sounds like a full day!"

"Yes, very. And it's only about halfway done."

"Tobias!" The man named Lucien stood up, walked over to Tobias, and shook hands with him. Lucien was slightly overweight, balding, with a mustache. He was wearing a dress shirt and khaki pants. He also smelled strongly of marijuana: it was an open secret that he partook in extracurricular activities outside of work, both for Bellwater Academy and the Bellwater Mages. Aurora didn't mind this as long as it didn't interfere with his work. Percival didn't care as long as parents didn't complain.

"Good afternoon, Lucien," Tobias said, smiling weakly at Lucien.

"Tobias, you simply must stop down to the art room sometime and see these medieval paintings the art students have come up with, they're just divine!"

Lucien had something of a reputation for being a bit pompous and overly polite to the other teachers. He thought it was a good way of making sure he maintained credibility to the other staff members.

"I'll have to check it out sometime, Lucien."

The four of them sat down and enjoyed lunch, discussing students, classes, and Agatha's unfortunate fall. Like Sabrina, Lucien shared the sentiment that Agatha's fall was a tragic accident. After the brief lunch, Tobias stopped at the men's restroom and relieved himself, then returned to classroom 18 and prepared for the next class period.

The tenth graders also started off amicably enough with the fifth hour, but halfway through the class, Tobias caught a student copying answers from another student. He confiscated the test and told the student that Mr. Ion would need to make the decision about a consequence for the student. Of course, this had a huge impact on the class, and arguing occurred throughout the rest of the period, which resulted in Tobias taking all of their tests from them and threatening to give them all zeros.

The study hall that came in during the sixth hour was off-the-walls wild. Half the class on the roster didn't show up, and the rest of them decided to play board games and chat loudly with each other as opposed to completing their homework. Tobias, who realized he was fighting a losing battle, let them do what they wanted; he was over it.

The last class of the day was public speaking, the elective class. Electives were typically more fun, laid-back classes, but this class was anything but. These students were exceptional—almost working too hard to try and one-up each other. Tobias left that class feeling like he himself could take lessons from the students despite the fact that he literally did public speaking for a living.

The end of the day had come at last. Tobias sighed and put his head in his hands. Teaching at Bellwater Academy always gave him a headache; this was something he was accustomed to, though it didn't really make him feel better.

"Long day?"

He looked up. It was Odion Montgomery, wearing a blue button-down shirt and tie that very closely matched what Tobias was wearing. His dress slacks were clean and neatly pressed, and his shirt and tie were ironed, making him look like a true professional. His dress shoes seemed to be freshly polished; it seemed like this was everyday wear for him.

"Yes, very. How was your day, Odion?" "Same as yours, I suppose."

Odion took a glance around the classroom, then entered the room and closed the door. "Tobias!" He whispered urgently. "Aurora told me–"

Tobias looked up, a look of warning in his eye. "Not here!" He said firmly.

"But–"

"No, Odion! Not here! Do you realize how dangerous it is to–"

"How dangerous it is to what?"

The door opened, and Percival Ion entered the room. His eyes scanned the room slowly as though looking for something–or someone. "Sorry to interrupt your conversation, gentlemen," he said, though he didn't sound sorry at all. "Tobias, I require a word. Odion, please leave us."

Odion left the classroom without another word to either Tobias or Percival. Percival closed the door. "Tobias, I heard you had an…interesting day."

Tobias looked at the principal. It was very unusual for him to stop by at the end of the day; something was up. "It was a hard day," he retorted after a few moments' silence.

"That it was, huh?" asked Percival. He sat down and looked at Tobias, his arms crossed. "Is there something that happened today that you wish to tell me about?"

"Should I start with the fist fight in the first hour, the threats made against another student in the second hour, or the cheating that happened in the fifth hour?"

"I'm most interested in the fourth hour, in fact."

Tobias looked at him. The fourth hour had been the seniors, his favorite class. The class with Foxton and Finnian.

"We discussed *Animal Farm*."

"Sounds to me like you had an agenda with that particular book."

"I beg your pardon?"

"Did you or did you not tell the students that 'humans are overworked, just like the horse, and we need to take a stand for ourselves'"?

"Yes, I did say that. Because that's what I believe."

Percival stood up. "Thank you for your work today, Tobias. We will not need you for substitute teaching moving forward."

"Um…sorry?"

"And you'll be reported to the state board of education for your comments."

Tobias stared at the principal.

"There will be a hearing…you may lose your teaching license…"

"Because I said that humans need to be protective of their time, and not give it all to the man?"

"Yes, Tobias. You cannot say those things to children."

Tobias and Percival stared at each other.

"You're joking," said Tobias calmly. "You wouldn't report me for something like this."

"Not joking, Tobias. I need to ask you to leave the premises. Gather your things! I'll escort you out."

Tobias stood up, and as he did so, the light overhead flickered. Tobias was angry; he was so angry right now at the situation. He couldn't believe this was happening. "So I'm getting fired over having an opinion? What happened to freedom of speech?"

Percival was looking at Tobias. He seemed to have noticed the lights flickering but didn't say anything; it was almost as though he had expected it.

"You are a teacher, Tobias. You don't have freedom of speech when in school."

At this, Tobias actually laughed. As he did so, he noticed that sparks were starting to fly around a nearby electrical outlet–the one housing Agatha's computer. He stopped laughing. He needed to control himself. Some things were more important than a teaching license.

"I'll show myself out, Percival. Didn't want to work for you anyway."

He grabbed his bag and walked out of the room, slamming the door shut on the way out.

Chapter Seven:
It's Time to Duel

"Calm down, Toby! It will be alright."

Tobias and Aurora were back in her cottage. Tobias was pacing the floor of Aurora's living room. He was livid that Percival had the audacity to fire him. Over what? Because he shared an opinion with his students?

"We are overworking ourselves to the point of exhaustion, Aurora! How does he not see that?!" he shouted.

"Yes, I know, Toby," she replied calmly. "It's just that some of the students thought you were trying to be political. I'm sure this whole thing will be smoothed over soon enough—"

"Well, I'm not, Aurora. I'm not going back to that school."

Aurora glared at Tobias. "Listen, Toby! I know you had a bad day, and I know you didn't want to go and sub there. But I need you to be able to—"

"No, Aurora. This is my choice. It's not up to you anymore."

Tobias and Aurora, who had always gotten along very well, now stood at opposite ends of the cottage's living room, glaring at each other. Tobias was furious. How could she stand there and defend the principal? How could she think it was right that he be expelled from the school while there were, at that very moment, teachers committing far more atrocious acts than he would ever dream of all around the world?

"I need some air," said Tobias. He turned and left the cottage abruptly before Aurora could stop him.

He teleported rather than walked to the clearing in the woods where he had taken the kids. Where he had brought Darian back to life–at great personal risk. Where he had brought the group after their school burned to the ground. He had sacrificed everything–everything–for the kids, and this is how they repaid him? He sat down next to the pond, and stared out into its depths, not saying anything, or even really thinking about anything.

What he wanted–what he really wanted–was to be done. He was in a very dark place. He had been here before, wanting to end his life rather than deal with the pain that everyday living brought him. Believing– genuinely believing– that the world would be a better place had he not been in it. What if another teacher had subbed in for Agatha? Would this whole thing have been avoided? Or would Percival have fired them too? At this moment, he wanted nothing more than to–

"Tobias?"

He turned and saw Odion Montgomery approaching

him with caution. "I…er…Aurora told me what happened," he said sheepishly. "Are you okay?"

Tobias scoffed and turned away from him. "What do you think, Odion? Why don't you try using your brain for a minute?"

He regretted his choice of words almost at once. There was a rather awkward and uncomfortable silence between the two men now. It was heavy, as though Tobias had suggested Odion try to drown himself.

"Sorry," he said quietly.

"That's quite all right," Odion replied. "That was…a stupid question. Of course, you're not okay."

"I always used to tell my students that there was no such thing as a stupid question. Just stupid answers."

"Oh, there's such a thing as a stupid question. A question is stupid if you're asking, and you already know the answer."

Tobias chuckled. "Yeah, I suppose that's true." "May I sit with you?"

"Sure, if you want. Not sure I'll be good company right now, though."

"I think you need it more than I do, Tobias."

Odion sat down next to Tobias. "Did Aurora put you up to this?"

"No, actually. She just said you had had a bad day." Tobias frowned. "Then why are you here?"

"What do you mean?"

"Odion, we've known each other for less than three days. Why are you coming out to comfort me?"

"Do you have an objection?" "No, but…it's kind of odd."

Odion shrugged. "I don't think it's odd," he retorted. "I think it's important to check on people. People need other people, Tobias. We all do. Life isn't something we can just do on our own. We rely on the people around us. Our friends, families, neighbors, even our colleagues. It would be very hard to do it alone."

"Yes, and yet I'm doing it alone."

"Why is that?"

"Because I don't need a therapist, Odion. I've always been alone. My whole life. I've never really had any friends other than Aurora, and she's…different. My parents died when I was young. Never really knew them. I bounced around in orphanages my whole childhood. Never staying in one spot for more than maybe a few months at most. In and out of foster care. Then, when I got into high school, Aurora found me and introduced me to magic."

Odion looked at Tobias. There was something weird about the look he was giving him. Then Tobias realized what it was: pity.

"I don't need your pity, Odion. I've long since accepted my role in society. I'm a loner. Always have been. Always will be."

"It does sound like you need a therapist, though, Toby."

"Please don't call me that."

Odion blinked. "Okay, Tobias. It does sound like you need a therapist."

Tobias looked away from him. "Yeah, probably. So, are you a therapist or something?"

"No, not quite. I actually would like to be your friend."

Tobias didn't say anything. He blinked, then looked around the clearing. "And why is that?" he said after several long minutes.

"Because I like you, Tobias. I think you're a great guy. I see how you are with Aurora. And you should hear Foxton and Finnian talk about you the last few days. They're staying with me at our safe house. They really respect and admire you."

"Yeah, well, none of that matters now, does it?"

"Of course it matters, Tobias. It makes all the difference in the world. You saved five innocent people from burning to death and put yourself at risk in the process. That's something to be proud of. That act of bravery, kindness, and selflessness should be admired. You should be proud of yourself, and others should be proud of you, too."

"Then why isn't Percival?"

Odion opened his mouth to retort, then quickly closed it again. Evidently, he wasn't sure how to answer.

"I think, Tobias," he said slowly and gently, "that Percival is trying to protect the school. He is putting the schools' needs above the needs of his staff."

"Oh, so he's like every other principal in the country?"

"It's not just education, you know. There are plenty of loser bosses outside of teaching, too."

Tobias sighed. "Yes, I suppose you're right about that."

The two men sat in silence for a long while. The wind picked up slightly; the trees began swaying, the leaves rustling around in the clearing. The pond looked like glass, smooth on the surface. The whole area was calm and peaceful.

"I quit my job today," Odion said to Tobias.

"You did what now?"

"I quit," said Odion, turning to Tobias.

"Why'd you do that?"

"Because Aurora said I'm going with you. On a mission."

Tobias turned away from him. He forgot that he had told Aurora he would babysit Odion on this trip, although he still wasn't sure it was the correct place for Odion.

"Want to tell me more about this mission?" "What do you want to know?"

"Well, what's the goal?"

"We are looking for someone."

"Who?"

Tobias hesitated, then realized something: if Odion was going to be joining him, there was no way he would be able to hide this from him.

"We are looking for my...friend, Hunter. He was last seen the day I brought those students here. He and two of his allies were burning down the school I was teaching at."

Odion frowned. "Why are we looking for him?"

"Because I think he's been forced to join the Arcane Rebellion."

"Forced to?"

"Yeah. I think someone—or something—is making him do things for the Rebellion he doesn't want to do."

"Like who?"

"Not sure, really."

Odion looked confused. "But isn't it impossible to force

people to do what you want them to do against their will, even with magic?"

"Kind of, yes. There's no using mind control or anything like that. But you can use your magic to coerce someone into telling the truth. Bully them, threaten them."

"But–correct me if I'm wrong–aren't spellcasters resistant to magic?"

"They're resistant to their own branch of magic. You can try and drown me in water all you want, but it won't work. I can breathe underwater. You can jolt me with a bolt of lightning; it'll tickle. But you can hit me with fire or with an earthquake or something."

"Or, you can use the elements to force something else to kill you."

"Correct. If you used water to propel a car forward and slammed into me with the car, you would hurt me. Just not from the water."

"So if Hunter is resistant to fire magic, it's gotta be someone who's not using fire magic, right?"

"Correct."

"I see. Well, that narrows it down a bit, doesn't it?"

"Not really. Most spellcasters have some degree of skill with various elements. I specialize in water, wind, and lightning. And there are many spellcasters who don't specialize in fire magic."

Tobias stood up suddenly.

"I want to see what you're capable of, Odion. Before I take you with me."

Odion stood up, too. He looked excited, ready to prove himself.

"Alright. What should I do?"

"Defend yourself."

The pond exploded. Water was gushing in highly pressurized jets towards Odion. It hit him square in the face, and he was pushed backward by the force of the water.

"You're not defending yourself, Odion!" Tobias called, smirking. He raised his hands, and the water from the pond leaped up and danced around Odion, soaking him head to toe.

Odion pointed directly at Tobias. The water stopped as suddenly as it had begun; it changed direction, now heading towards Tobias, who was ready for it. He clapped his hands, and a strong gust of wind tore directly down the middle of the jet of water flying towards him. The water flew right past him, on either side of Tobias, but the wind went right through the water. Odion got swept up in the wind, and flew backward into a tree. He slammed into the tree hard. Leaves, acorns, and even a squirrel fell from the tree and hit Odion in the head; the squirrel ran away quickly, obviously terrified of the fighting men.

Odion teleported away from the tree and directly behind Tobias. However, Tobias had been expecting this; he turned around instantly, slamming his fists down to his side. He was surrounded by rushing winds on all sides. The water that Odion sent back towards Tobias simply blew away, back into the pond, where it lay motionless. Tobias waved his hands in a fluid, circular motion; instantly, Odion was swept up into a small tornado, which ripped through the clearing, uprooting trees and grass. Odion screamed, not able to stop the flow of the wind.

Tobias lowered his hands, and the wind stopped. Odion fell to the ground, panting. "You win! I surrender! Uncle, uncle!"

"It was not about winning or losing, Odion," said Tobias briskly. "I...am not impressed with you, if I'm being honest. I realize I took you by surprise, but you really should have been able to fight back a bit better than that. If I were an enemy magician, you'd be dead."

Tobias waved his hands over the surface of the clearing. All of the water from the pond flew back to its rightful place, the trees rooted themselves back into their homes, and the grass seemed to regrow as suddenly as it had been ripped out of the ground.

Tobias went and sat next to Odion. It was several long minutes before Odion had caught his breath and recomposed himself.

"I'm sorry," he said after a while.

"Don't be sorry. Be better." Tobias spoke calmly and patiently for someone who had just commanded the elements to attack this man.

"I will. I just need more practice."

"I know. You're new. But this isn't going to be some walk in the park, Odion. This is potentially a dangerous mission. It involves infiltrating the Arcane Rebellion. And I need to know: are you ready for this? Are you ready to die to serve our cause?"

"Yes, Tobias. I am."

"Why, Odion?"

Odion hesitated, then said quietly, "Because I have to."

"And why's that?"

"I…I would rather not say."

"Oh, come on. I shared with you."

"I'll keep that information to myself for now."

Tobias nodded, recognizing the dismissal. "Okay. Well, we should probably be getting back. Aurora's probably worried sick about me by now."

They stood up. Tobias reached out a hand towards Odion.

"Hey, real quick. Thanks for coming out here tonight. I do appreciate it, even if I have a weird way of showing it."

Odion smiled. "Of course, Tobias. But can I call you Toby now?"

Tobias laughed. "Sure, if that's what you want."

Then, Odion did something that Tobias wasn't

expecting. Tobias had been holding out his hand, ready for a firm handshake, but Odion instead grabbed his arm and pulled him towards him into a hug.

"Is this okay?"

"Yeah, sure, Odion."

Tobias reached around and hugged Odion back. He had hugged people before, of course, but never quite like this. Odion was holding on to him as though he were something of value that he didn't want to lose. The hug stretched on for seconds, then minutes. It was strange for Tobias at first, but he eventually started to really appreciate the hug. After about two minutes, they let go of each other. Tobias had let go of Odion first, he noticed.

"Thanks, Toby."

Odion turned and vanished into midair. Tobias stood in the clearing, all alone. It was pretty obvious to Tobias that Odion had needed that hug more than he needed it.

Chapter Eight:
Gathering of Great Minds

The next morning, Tobias awoke in Aurora's guest bedroom. He had snuck in and avoided her throughout the night, but it was time to talk to her about what happened yesterday.

Aurora was sitting at the table, drinking a cup of coffee, and reading a book. She looked up as Tobias walked in.

"Toby!"

"Good morning, Aurora," he said, helping himself to a seat. "I just wanted to say I'm sorry for how I reacted yesterday. I shouldn't have taken it out on you."

Aurora put down her book, carefully marking the place where she was. Then she turned to Tobias.

"Listen, Toby. I know you had a terrible day yesterday—"

"Understatement of the year."

"—but I think you should consider calling Percival and talking things through with him."

Tobias stared at her.

"You do understand what happened, right Aurora? I got fired. I didn't quit. I didn't walk out. I was asked to leave."

"Yes, well, I still think it'd be worth a try."

"Actually, Aurora, Odion came to see me last night."

"Oh?"

"Yeah. We talked, and I think I'm going to enjoy having him tag along with me as we find Hunter."

Aurora sighed. "I knew you'd say something like that," she replied. "Listen…"

She pulled herself up to her full height. "Before you go…we are having a staff meeting here in about an hour."

Tobias frowned. "A staff meeting? At the cottage?"

"Yes. The school isn't safe for us at the moment. Percival has been…unkind to several of us in the last few weeks. It's rather odd. He's never been like this before, not allowing us to have our meetings or anything at the school."

The spellcasters of Bellwater Academy had set it up to where they had a "teacher's union" meeting about once a month. This union meeting was actually a meeting for the spellcasters to discuss current events going on at and outside of the school. It had never really been an issue for Bellwater Academy before, so it was concerning that

Percival was starting to crack down on these meetings.

"I see. And let me guess. You'd like me to attend."

"Well…yes, Toby. I think it'd be good for you to get a feel for where we are at before you and Odion depart."

Tobias grinned at her. "Of course, you're absolutely right, as usual, Aurora. I'll have a quick breakfast if that's ok?"

"Of course, Toby. Help yourself!"

She reached into the pantry and pulled out a box of cereal and some bananas. Tobias grabbed bowls and spoons. They spent the next hour or so enjoying each other's company over a lowkey breakfast, laughing with each other, catching up on old times and happy memories.

Then, there was a knock on the door. Tobias finished cleaning up the kitchen while Aurora went to answer it. Five people entered the cottage.

The first was Agatha O'Connor, the English teacher Tobias had substituted for. An elderly woman with a broken hip, she walked on crutches and was moving very slowly.

Magic was not something that could be used to heal things like illness or wounds. Generally speaking, magic could be used like one would use a gun or a knife - you could defend yourself with it or attack someone with it. But beyond teleportation, scrying, resurrection, and a few other niche circumstances, magic wasn't something you could just use to fix anything and everything. It certainly made some things easier, although it also made things significantly more challenging if it was misused.

There was one notable exception to this: magic could be used to heal wounds caused by magic. This is why Tobias had been able to resurrect Darian a few days prior. As Agatha had fallen, she couldn't use her magic to heal her broken hip.

"Tobias!" Agatha greeted him. He smiled at her. "You sub for me for one day and get fired? It was that bad, was it?"

"Oh, it was just Percival, Agatha. Nothing to take personally."

"Oh, but I do, Tobias. You see, because there's no sub, I had to go back to work three weeks earlier than I had planned! How am I supposed to teach like this?"

Tobias was stunned. "He's making you go back? Already?"

"Yes, Tobias. Are you really surprised? It's not like there's a surplus of teachers."

"But you need time to heal!"

"Doesn't matter to that old fool. Parents and the school board come first, students second, and staff members last. Remember?"

Tobias smiled at her sadly. "I'm sorry, Agatha."

"Oh, don't be! I knew it was a matter of time. He never

did like you." She pulled him into a whisper; for having a broken hip, she had a surprising amount of strength. "And he likes me well enough that I can just sit at my desk and have the kids watch movies. It's really not a big deal, honey."

She smiled at him and walked into the living room, where she took the nearest armchair near the door.

Tobias smiled back at her and turned to face the next person entering the cottage. A tall, blonde woman was up next. She had her hair up in a ponytail, and was wearing an elegant red sweater, blue jeans, and deep red lipstick.

"Good morning, Sabrina," Tobias greeted her politely.

"Oh, good morning, Tobias. I wasn't expecting to see you here."

"Yes, well, you know how Aurora is. Wouldn't take no for an answer."

"I see. Yes, she is rather persistent, isn't she?"

Sabrina walked into the living room and took the chair furthest from the door. Tobias turned to see Lucien Rodgson, the music and art teacher, enter the cottage.

"Good morning, Lucien."

"Oh, hello, Tobias. I heard about the…er…incident at the school with Percival. I'm sorry that happened to you. That's rotten luck."

"Yes, thank you, Lucien."

Lucien shook hands with Tobias, then walked and took the seat next to Sabrina.

Odion was the next to enter the cottage. He, too, smiled at Tobias, shaking hands with him before sitting next to Agatha.

The final person to enter the cottage was Matilda Carrington.

"Hello Tobias!" she greeted in a friendly manner.

"Hello, Matilda! Come on in!"

Matilda thanked Tobias and took the seat next to Sabrina and Lucien. This left Tobias to sit next to Odion and Agatha. Aurora entered the room last and sat down in the chair in the center of the room, facing out towards everyone.

"Thank you all for coming! I realize it's been some time since our last meeting. We have…quite a few things to cover today. Let's start with updates on how training the students is going!"

She turned to Matilda. "Matilda, your update, please! How are the new students doing?"

"All over the place," said Matilda. "Foxton and Finnian seem to be adjusting relatively well. Foxton is eager and ready to learn. Finnian is too, though is definitely feeling a bit more…in shock…about the events that transpired earlier this week." She glanced at Tobias at these words. "Lyra and Elena, the female twins, aren't doing as well. They are in a constant state of anxiety, I fear. They keep looking over their shoulders, expecting someone to be attacking them, or something. And then the boy called Darian is...well, he seems to be in shock as well. He has taken to isolating himself from the others and even broke off his relationship with Elena."

Tobias was saddened to hear that not all of his former students were excelling in their new roles, though he was also not entirely surprised. After all, they had been uprooted against their will into this new life. He also thought about how he had been upset, back in the clearing the day before, that Lyra, Elena, and Darian didn't seem to want anything to do with him and chalked it up to them simply going through a lot.

Aurora nodded. "Do you feel that Foxton and Finnian are ready for advancement?" "Yes,

I do."

"Okay. Sabrina, please take over the training of these students from Matilda."

"Understood," said tall, blonde Sabrina, taking notes on her notepad as she spoke.

"I know you have no students under your charge at this point, Sabrina, so we will skip you and go right to Lucien." She turned to the man sitting to Sabrina's right. "Updates for us on your apprentices?"

"Both of them seem to be doing well," he replied curtly. "Nikola has taken to the power of fire and is ready for advancement–probably to you, Sabrina. Garth has excelled in the art of wind magic and is also ready for advancement. To myself, I presume, Aurora?"

"Yes, that would be fine," Aurora said curtly, making a note on her clipboard.

Each of the teachers specialized in their own elements. Tobias specialized in and typically taught lightning magic, Sabrina taught fire magic, Aurora taught earth magic, Agatha taught water magic, and Lucien taught wind magic. Matilda's role focused more on the new students and bringing them up to speed on every aspect of their lives as a spellcaster. Typically, students began studying with Matilda, and then would be assigned another of the spellcasters prior to choosing their specialization. Garth and Nikola had begun training with Matilda, then went to Lucien, and now were ready for more advanced training. Odion, being brand new, wasn't teaching just yet.

"Agatha, any updates? I know you are out of commission right now."

"I have no apprentices. Apparently, these students don't understand the nuances of water magic."

"Well, even if they did, Agatha, you are in no fit state to teach them," replied Aurora curtly.

"I'll try and help some of these new ones see the beauty of water," said Sabrina kindly to Agatha. "It is beautiful, isn't it?"

"You would say that, you fire-eater, wouldn't you?"

"Agatha!" said Aurora warningly. But Sabrina

laughed. "Oh, don't worry about it, Aurora!"

"Moving on, then," said Aurora quickly before Agatha could respond. "Odion, how is your training going?"

Odion glanced quickly at Tobias, then said quickly, "Quite well, I think. We started last night."

"Oh? And how did it go?"

Odion hesitated, and then Tobias spoke. "He did fine. Some work to be done, of course. But nothing Odion can't handle."

Odion grinned at Tobias. Aurora made a check on her clipboard.

"Alright, then, the next order of business is this darn Arcane Rebellion."

Aurora pulled out several sheets of paper and passed them out. They were drawings done of a seemingly large base of operations. "I have found where they are shored up, or at least a group of them. They are to the south, off a beach in Florida. I am sending Tobias to investigate, along with Odion."

The group looked surprised at this news. "Why is that?" asked Matilda curiously.

"Tobias feels the need to investigate what the Arcane Rebellion is up to," said Aurora.

Tobias nodded. They had spoken, over breakfast, about the need to keep the true reason for Tobias' mission under wraps, even from the other teachers.

"After what happened to those students...I need answers. They need answers," Tobias provided helpfully.

The other teachers nodded and smiled at him in understanding.

Aurora said, "My sources tell me this is one of their main bases of operation, and where they conduct a large amount of business. This should hit them where it hurts."

"Well, that brings us to our final point, and why we are all here today: Percival Ion."

There was an immediate shift in the atmosphere of the room. It was as though Aurora had uttered a profane word that had offended everyone in the vicinity.

"I know he's been getting on all of you lately," began Aurora.

"Understatement of the year," said Lucien to several nods of agreement.

"Yes," said Aurora, frowning. "I am trying to discover the reason for this. He's never been like this before. Even Beatrice is at a loss and has noticed."

"You don't think he knows about us, do you?" Asked Sabrina, sounding worried.

"No, I don't think so," replied Aurora reassuringly. "I think if he knew about us, we'd know." Sabrina sighed with a sense of relief.

"For the time being, your orders are to stand down and let him do what he wants."

"And if we all get fired?" asked Matilda. "Isn't that what happened to Tobias?"

"We will cross that bridge if we come to it," said Aurora calmly. "Don't forget! If Percival Ion starts acting against us, we can always…act, if need be."

Everyone in the room understood "act" to mean "kill him where he stands with the full might of the elements." It didn't need to be said out loud.

"But for the time being, I feel that would draw unwanted attention to us. Tobias and Percival have history, and Tobias was, for all intents and purposes, only a substitute teacher. If he goes after any of you–" she nodded to each of the teachers in the room, "--I will personally take care of it. Understood?"

They all nodded.

"Excellent. Then, you are all dismissed. We will meet again in a few weeks."

One by one, the teachers left. Soon, it was just Tobias, Aurora, and Odion.

"Odion, we will leave tomorrow," said Tobias. "Go, rest, relax, and be prepared to leave at sunrise tomorrow. Meet here, at the cottage. We will have a big day ahead of us."

Odion nodded and walked out the front door with the

other teachers.

"You know," said Tobias thoughtfully, "I think I'm really going to like him."

Chapter Nine:
Departure

Odion arrived at the cottage the next day, and Tobias answered the door. Odion was wearing his usual dress shirt and tie, dress slacks, and black dress shoes. Tobias was wearing a hoodie and sweatpants.

"G'Morning, Toby!" greeted Odion cheerfully. He walked into the cottage and closed the door behind him.

Tobias looked Odion up and down and asked, "Why are you dressed up so much?"

"It's a beautiful day! I always feel my best when I'm dressed up!"

"It's six o'clock in the morning."

"Yes, but even so," Odion turned to look at Tobias, "We have a big day ahead of us today, don't we?!"

"I don't know what you think we'll be doing," replied Tobias curtly. "Comfort is more important than style for our mission."

"Yes, but even so, a little style never went amiss."

Tobias avoided rolling his eyes with extreme difficulty

but said nothing more about the subject and escorted Odion into the dining room. Aurora was sitting at the table in a nightgown, drinking a cup of coffee and eating a bowl of cereal.

"Ah, good morning, Odion! I see you're...dressed up?"

"Yes, Aurora. It's important to leave a good first impression!"

"We've met before," Tobias reminded him. "Yes, but I like dressing up."

Aurora chuckled as Tobias really did roll his eyes this time, albeit while Odion was looking at Aurora.

"So, how long do you need, Toby?" asked Odion. "What do you mean?"

"I mean, how long until you're ready to go?" "I'm ready now."

Odion stared at him. "I...see." He looked up and down at Tobias' clothing of choice. "And that's...all you're bringing?"

"I have a backpack. How about you?"

Odion went back outside and opened the door, carrying two large backpacks inside with him. Tobias blanched.

"Yeah...you're gonna need to bring less stuff."

"How long will we be gone?"

"Dunno. Days? Weeks? Months? I couldn't even begin to guess."

"And you want me to only bring one backpack?" "It's not like there aren't laundromats, Odion."

"Yes, but...we're spellcasters! Surely we don't use normal things like laundromats?"

"Yes, we do," Aurora chimed in. "It's actually imperative to our survival. This isn't a fairytale, Odion. We live alongside–and in harmony with–people who don't practice magic. Why do you think we all have 'real' jobs?"

"Some would argue teaching isn't a real job," Tobias pointed out. Aurora ignored him.

"Speaking of teaching," Odion began, but Aurora cut him off.

"I've worked it all out with Percival. We have a substitute lined up for you. I managed to turn your resignation into a temporary leave of absence."

"Oh, sure, now there are plenty of substitutes, eh?"

"Yes, well, now that Agatha is back at work–"

"--which is silly, if you ask me–"

"Yes, I agree, Toby. But I can't pretend it doesn't help us out a bit."

Tobias nodded but didn't say anything. No matter what he said to the contrary, what had happened with his teaching career still really hurt him. Tobias had always enjoyed teaching, even if it wasn't his idea of a good time all the time.

"Well, regardless. Odion, leave one of the backpacks here!"

Rather reluctantly, Odion brought one of his backpacks to Aurora's spare bedroom—which evidently had only carried extra clothes--then returned to the dining room.

"Alright, Odion. Here's the plan. We are going to teleport to a small beach about 50 miles from the port where the Arcane Rebellion is holed up."

"Why don't we just teleport directly to the port?"

"For a few reasons," said Aurora briskly. "For one, the Arcane Rebellion will be on the lookout for enemy mages and will not respond well to you guys teleporting directly into their base of operations. For two, it is unlikely that you would be able to. Remember, you can block teleportation in certain areas, like this cottage."

"So, what's our plan of attack? 50 miles is a long walk."

"About a mile off the beach is a car dealership. Aurora has generously given us funds to rent a car."

"Ok...so we'll drive in? I fail to see how that's better than teleporting in."

"We will drive to the port disguised as workers," said Tobias calmly. "There's a cruise ship that operates out of that port. I have arranged for two of the workers to be unable to work for a while. We have been hired as their temporary replacements."

Odion frowned. "You killed them, Toby?"

"No, no, of course not! I simply flooded their house. They are husband and wife."

"Oh, is that all?"

"Fear n o t . I t r i p l e -checked, and they have homeowners' insurance with flood protection."

"How in the world did you manage that?"

"I hacked into the insurance companies database and verified their policies. And I did it again last night. They've filed a claim, and it's been approved. They're just awaiting payment."

"You know how to hack?"

"I'm…rather good with computers, Odion."

"I suppose it helps, when you're using a computer to do some hacking, to have the ability to short-circuit the computer with a snap of your fingers?"

"Actually, not as much as you might think. Don't fall into the trap that so many of us fall into when we first start practicing magic, Odion. Magic isn't all that powerful. You still need to rely on the skills you learned prior to becoming a mage for some things."

"He's right, you know," said Aurora gently. "Magic often can do much more harm than good. I've seen it first- hand."

Odion said nothing but contemplated this. He supposed it made sense that magic was only as powerful as the person using it.

"Any other questions?"

"Yes. What will we do when we get there?"

"Well, with any luck, we'll manage to enter the facility undetected. They do have mostly non-magic folks working there at this point. And our names are in the database, so we should be good there. But as far as once we're inside…well, we need to try to find the rebellion's base of operations. That's not going to be easy, and it's certainly not going to be a place we have access to."

"My scrying has indicated no hints as to where it could be either. My guess is it is somewhere underground. I was able to scry everywhere within the port until I tried scrying the basement. But that part of the port is undetectable. I would guess that they've set up the basement to act as their base. You need to try and get down there."

"Now, this is really important, Odion. We cannot kill anyone while we're there. Not even members of the rebellion. We don't want to draw unwanted attention to ourselves."

"Understood."

"No, I want this to be crystal clear. You are not to kill anyone, or be killed. And we are not to use magic unless it is absolutely necessary. And even then, we are only to use magic to get ourselves out as quickly as possible."

"Okay. I get it."

"Alright," Tobias nodded. "Are you ready? Any other questions?"

"Nope. I think I'm ready."

The three of them walked outside to the front yard after Tobias and Odion swung their backpacks on.

"Good luck, you two!" said Aurora, hugging Tobias and Odion both in turn. Odion sunk into the hug a bit longer than was necessary. Aurora pulled away, looking a little concerned. "Er–I will see you both soon."

"Bye, Aurora!" said Tobias, smiling at her.

He and Odion teleported into nothing. They reappeared on a small, sandy beach. The weather was surprisingly cool on the beach; the sun had barely risen, and it was looking to be a rather cloudy, overcast day. The two of them stared out into the ocean for a short while, then began walking towards the dealership that Tobias had mentioned.

With it being so early in the morning, no one was really out and about. They passed a few runners on their walk to the dealership but no one else. They didn't really talk much either; instead, they walked in silence, taking in their surroundings. It was unseasonably cold.

After about ten minutes, they were walking up to the door of the dealership. They entered and were instantly greeted by a short, squat man with a suit.

"Hello!" said Tobias politely. "We are here about the car rental. The reservation is under 'Tobias.'"

"Yes, here you are. Just sign here…and here…oh, and here too! You should be all set. Enjoy the ride!"

The two men left the dealership, put their backpacks into the car, and drove away. The car was a blue sedan with four doors; it was completely inconspicuous. Tobias had begged Aurora to let him get a convertible, but Aurora had—rightly—told him no, that it would be too easily recognized and would stand out too much.

The first fifteen or twenty minutes of the drive were met with silence between the two men. Tobias actually thought for a moment that Odion had fallen asleep. But then, Odion broke the silence.

"Why did you become a spellcaster?"

The question was so simple, and yet so unexpected that Tobias was startled by it. It took him a moment to regain his composure and respond.

"It was actually because of my friend, Hunter." "The one we're looking for?"

"The very same."

"You must really care for him."

"I do," whispered Tobias, so quietly that he wasn't sure Odion could hear him. "How about you? Why did you become a spellcaster?"

"I didn't even know about it two months ago. I just graduated from college. Math education major. Math teachers are needed everywhere, but I couldn't find a job to save my life. Finally, Percival gave me a chance. I don't think he had a choice; I was the only option."

"That doesn't answer my question."

"I know. I'm just giving you some context. Anyway, on my first day of in-service, Aurora walked up to me and said that she wanted to meet with me in private. I thought this can't be good. The guidance counselor wanted to meet with me on my first day?"

"And she told you about magic?" Tobias was surprised; this was rather unlike Aurora.

"Not exactly," said Odion sheepishly. "I kind of…followed her to her cottage. She said she wanted to meet with me, so I went to her cottage."

"That's kinda…creepy."

"Yeah, well, never mind that. I saw her out in her garden, and she was making her vegetables grow so quickly. Too quickly. I knew something was up. I asked her what she was doing, and how she was doing it. Well, at first, she was playing dumb. 'What are you talking about? I'm just gardening' kind of thing, but I kept asking. And eventually, she gave in and showed me her trick.

Then I asked her if she could teach me. Tell you the truth, I think she was half expecting to kill me."

"She probably was."

"That doesn't make me feel better."

"Nor should it. Aurora is a very private person. I'm surprised she didn't make a carrot grow out of your—"

"Yes, well, moving past that. Tell me about Hunter!"

"What do you want to know?"

"How long have you known him?"

"We were best friends in high school." "Were?

Are you not anymore?"

"It's…complicated." "We've

got time."

Tobias sat in silence for a few minutes, pondering his answer. How did he explain the friendship he and Hunter had to someone who was, until quite recently, a complete stranger? He hardly knew Odion; it had been less than a week since they had met. And yet here he was, almost a complete stranger, asking him questions about Hunter.

Hunter…

"Sorry, Toby. If you don't want to talk about it, we can talk about something else."

Tobias turned to look at him. Odion was smiling at him. It was quite obvious to him that Odion cared about him.

"Can I ask you something, then?" "Of

course."

"Why do you care so much about me?"

Odion looked puzzled, and a little hurt.

"I don't mean to be rude," said Tobias quickly. "But we barely know each other. We met less than a week ago, Odion. And you're asking me questions about my past like we're best friends. Are you always like this?"

"Er–yes, actually. As a matter of fact, it's gotten me into some trouble in the past. I don't know when to stop. People seem to like me a lot less than I like them."

That last statement took Tobias by surprise. "People seem to like you a lot less than you like them? What does that even mean?"

"I thought it was quite clear, actually. I love people. I enjoy their company. I love making people happy. People, for whatever reason, don't seem to reciprocate that feeling towards me."

"Well, I'm sorry to hear that."

"I'm not," said Odion tactfully. "It's something I've learned to accept and live with. It's not…ideal by any stretch of the imagination. But it could be worse. Better to love too much than not enough."

"It doesn't mean that you don't get hurt, though."
"That's true. But what's life without getting hurt?"

Tobias considered this for a moment. What's life without getting hurt? What a stupid thing to think, was his initial thought. But the more he thought about it, the more it seemed to make sense.

His fallout with Hunter, and the fight they had consumed so much of his energy and feelings towards the man that he had almost forgotten all of the good things that had happened before their fight. The days they'd skip school and play sports or games. The days they'd drive around recklessly. The long nights they'd spend with each other, sitting around talking. Telling stories. Just enjoying each other's company.

The truth was, Tobias had never had a friend quite like Hunter. He and Hunter were often mistaken for brothers because of how often they were together, how similar they were in personality, and how much they adored each other. It was quite obvious to anyone who was paying attention, Aurora often said.

Would he actually be willing to give all of that up? All of those happy memories, all of those good times? It was hard getting past their last interaction, and yet, he wasn't sure he could give up all of the times they had prior. Was the bad memory worth giving up all of the good memories?

"You okay, Toby?"

Tobias looked around. Odion was staring at him, a little concerned.

"You've been staring off into space for a long time. Are you even paying attention to the road?"

Tobias grinned at him. "Of course I am, don't be silly!"

Tobias glanced at the road and paid attention for the first time in what felt like hours. Tobias didn't drive much, and it had been a while. But he was confident that he would safely get himself and Odion to the port.

They sat in silence for the rest of the drive. Tobias was thinking hard about everything Odion had said. He didn't even register that he had just pulled into a parking lot.

"Hey, Odion?"

Odion looked around.

"Thanks for coming!"

"Of course! Wouldn't miss it." "Well,

good. Cause we're here."

Chapter Ten:
Cruising for a Bruising

Tobias looked around as he and Odion got out of the car. They were in a large parking lot that had about half the parking spaces occupied by a variety of vehicles. They were parked facing the ocean, with a pier directly in front of them. This pier was big enough to house an entire cruise ship. While there was no cruise ship in port at the moment, it was obvious there was to be one arriving later that day; people had already started lining up at the terminal, and Tobias could only assume they were there to board the ship.

To the right of the pier was a big building that looked like a warehouse from a distance. Upon closer inspection, it seemed to be serving a dual purpose of both warehouse and cruise ship check-in area for passengers to check themselves in for their vacations. Tobias went around to the back of the car while Odion continued to survey his surroundings.

"Here, I have something for you."

Tobias pulled his backpack out from the trunk of the car and removed two uniforms. They looked like typical cruise ship deckhand uniforms. Odion frowned.

"So we have to change?"

"Yes, we do."

Tobias began undressing. A short, thin man, there was nothing out of the ordinary about him undressing. Odion, however, hesitated.

"What's up? Too afraid to show me that perfect body?"

"Oh, shut up, Toby!"

Odion, too, began changing. It felt weird to change in the middle of a parking lot in broad daylight, though they both kept their undergarments on. Their shirt and pants were removed and replaced with the uniform Tobias had provided. Then, Tobias pulled out two pairs of black shoes and slipped a pair onto his feet. Odion did the same.

Tobias and Odion looked each other up and down.

"Well, we should pass for deckhands. At least until we open our mouths."

Tobias pulled out his cellphone and checked the time. His cellphone was little more than a timepiece for him, but it was still nice to have, he supposed.

"About five minutes before our shift starts. Perfect! Are you ready to go?" "Yeah, I suppose."

Odion looked a little uncertain. Tobias looked at him.

"What's wrong?"

"It's just...this feels weird."

"That you're not dressed up?"

"No...it feels strange. To be here. Like we're 'undercover cops' or something."

"Being undercover isn't an easy thing," offered Tobias gently. "It takes some getting used to. I've done it for years."

Odion took a deep breath and nodded.

"Alright, let's go check it out. Let me do the talking."

The two men walked up to the building and entered through the front door.

The lobby of the building was large and spacious, quite the opposite of the front office of Bellwater Academy. It was warm in the building, a nice contrast to the chilly September morning air from outside. There were several chairs lined up against the walls, and in the middle of the room was a circular desk where a young receptionist sat.

"Good morning! Ah, you must be our new deckhands," she said warmly, smiling at them. She pointed at a door to her right. "If you go in through that door, Bill will help you out."

She smiled at them again and went back to her computer, typing. The two men walked to the door and pulled it open. They stepped inside a small hallway, quite in contrast to the large reception area they had just left. It was so dark in the room they needed to take a moment to allow their eyes to adjust to the change. Then, they began walking. It didn't take them long to reach another desk, this time with a young man with short, red hair and an earring seated behind it.

"Good morning," he said, not unkindly, though not quite as warmly as the young receptionist had greeted them. "May I help you?"

"Yes, we're here for work," Tobias replied a little nervously. It was normal to be nervous on your first day of work. He had to play the part.

"Ah, so you're..?"

"Tobias, sir."

"Please, none of that 'sir' nonsense. It's Bill. I'll be helping you out. And you are..?"

"Odion."

"Ah, nice to meet you. If the two of you could come this way."

Bill led them down the hallway a little bit more and into a small conference room. There was a round table in a small meeting room; the room could only house maybe three or four people.

"We have some documents for you to sign, and then a training video for you to watch," said Bill. He pointed towards a small television that was hooked up to the wall. It had a built-in DVD player and looked like it had come from the mid-2000s.

"Er...before we start. Where is the nearest bathroom?" Tobias asked.

"Down the hall to your left."

"Thank you. Odion, do you need to come too? We've had a long drive, Bill." He gave Odion a piercing look.

"Yes, I do."

The two men left Bill in the conference room and walked quickly down the hall.

"Take a look around," whispered Tobias. "Any door, window, anything you see that could bring us to the basement."

The two men walked quickly, checking every door they passed. There were lots of conference rooms, and several offices, and they found the bathroom they had been instructed to go to but quickly passed it. They were on high alert, waiting for someone to discover them. Their biggest concern was Bill coming to find them, but he didn't come, so they continued their search.

"Toby!" Odion said in a loud, urgent whisper a few minutes later. "We're kind of striking out a bit here."

"Yes, I realize this," said Tobias. He sighed. They had one door left to check; if this door wasn't what they were looking for, they'd have to turn around and go back to Bill.

Tobias put his hand on the doorknob and turned. But it was locked. Tobias frowned. The door was solid, so he couldn't even look through the window.

"What now, Toby?"

"Magic."

"But you said no magic unless we are dying."

"Yes, well, rules are meant to be broken, aren't they?"

Tobias flicked his wrist towards the doorknob. A small jolt of electricity hit the locking mechanism; it turned, and the door was unlocked instantly.

"Whoa!" said Odion, impressed. "I didn't know electricity could do that."

"Electricity is my personal favorite of the elements for a reason, Odion. But water has its own share of tricks, too."

The two men opened the door silently so as not to be discovered. There was a small landing, and stairs leading downstairs. It was very dark, even darker than in the hallway. Odion frowned.

"How will we see..?"

"Never mind that. Just get in."

They entered through the doorway, Tobias closing the door behind him. A small click sound registered with Tobias; the door was locked behind them. Good, he thought. This way, they wouldn't be followed in here by Bill.

"Do you want me to go first, or do you want to go first,

Odion?"

"You go first."

"Scared of the dark, are we?"

"Little bit," admitted Odion.

"That's alright. We're all scared of something. The unknown scares us most of all."

Odion nodded. Tobias led the way, feeling his way down the stairs. Odion followed. The stairs were narrow, yet the slope was steep. They walked down the stairs for what seemed like a long time before Tobias stopped suddenly. Odion nearly bumped into him.

"Quiet!" whispered Tobias, listening hard. Odion listened, too.

There were two men up ahead. Tobias' heart sank; he recognized their voices. It was Hunter and the other man who had been with Hunter during the attack on Jefferson High.

"They killed Avery, Hunter! They killed him! What do you expect me to do, sit back and let them do their thing? I want revenge, Hunter!"

"Yes, I understand that, Ted. I want revenge, too. But attacking Bellwater Academy is not the answer."

"And why's that?"

"Because the majority of people at that school aren't

mages. They don't appreciate the work we do. And the ones who are mages are…well, they're really strong, Ted. You know how difficult it would be to kill them all? It's not like that other school we hit."

"But don't you think it's possible they have those new recruits that you've been keeping an eye on? Let's just go get 'em, Hunter! It'll be easy."

"The two of us attack a school that has multiple mages in both their students and teachers? It would be a suicide mission, Ted."

"Maybe some of the others would join in?"

"Like who? Avery's gone."

"How about that Marina?"

"Eh. I've never liked her. Water isn't really my thing."

The two men had started walking, it seemed; their voices were growing distant, and Tobias heard footsteps walking away from them.

"Toby!" whispered Odion in a hushed voice. "They're going to attack the school, Toby!"

"Hold on!" breathed Tobias. "That can't be their only plan, Odion."

Tobias turned to Odion. "Do you trust me?"

"Yes."

"Okay."

Tobias pointed a finger at a nearby light fixture. It was off but flashed for a quick second before turning off again. Then, images swirled in both Tobias's and Odion's minds. There were several rooms, all of them completely empty apart from a bed and dressers. It appeared these were sleeping quarters for people. A long hallway where two men were walking, facing backward away from the front of the basement. They saw the two men enter their living quarters, apparently going to bed for the night. Then there was one room, an office.

At the sight of the office, the swirling images stopped as suddenly as they had started. Odion looked puzzled by what had happened.

"I scryed the place. Odion. We're alone except for those two."

"How did you do that? I thought Aurora said we couldn't scry down here."

"Distance matters in magic, Odion. She was much farther away than we were. And protective enchantments can't protect this place from our scrying when we are actually down here."

"Ah, I see. So we only need to worry about Ted and Hunter?"

"Yes, but don't underestimate them! I don't know much about Ted, but Hunter is a powerful mage. I'd rather not fight them; let's be stealthy."

Odion nodded. The two men tiptoed slowly into the office where Ted and Hunter had been before. The office was small and cramped, but tidy. In the corner of the room was a desk with a computer on it.

"Ah!"

Tobias walked quickly, but quietly over to the desk, sat down, and started typing on the computer. It was locked and required a password. Tobias started looking around the desk.

"What are you doing?"

"I'm going to hack this computer."

"But you're not typing–"

"It'll be faster if I find the password this way, Odion. Trust me."

Tobias opened the drawers of the desk and found a small, black notebook labeled "Passwords."

"Typical," Tobias chuckled. He opened the notebook to the last page and found the last written password: P@ssword1! He typed it in. Instantly, he had full access to their files and documents.

"Just a second."

Tobias pulled his cellphone and a cord out of his pocket. He plugged the cord into the computer tower, then plugged the other end of his phone into the cord. Then he pressed a few buttons on the computer, and all of the files and documents from the computer started downloading directly onto his cellphone.

While Tobias was doing that, Odion was standing at the door of the room. He kept watch for any sign of Ted or Hunter coming down the hallway, but all was calm. Then Tobias whispered, "Yes!" and disconnected his cord from the computer.

"We got what we needed, Odion. Let's go!"

The two men left the office and slowly crept back up the stairs. It didn't seem to take nearly as much time to go back up as opposed to how long it took to get down.

Then, a man's voice blared over what appeared to be a loudspeaker throughout the entire building. Tobias recognized the man's voice: it was Bill's voice.

"Tobias Thornfield and Odion Montgomery, please report back to the conference room! Tobias Thornfield and Odion Montgomery, back to the conference room!"

Tobias gasped and tackled Odion to the ground. Then they teleported away.

Chapter Eleven:
Personal Attacks

Tobias and Odion appeared in the clearing near Bellwater Cottage. It was late afternoon; several hours seemed to have passed since they entered the cruise ship warehouse. Tobias was sweating profusely; it seemed this distant teleportation had taken a great toll on him.

"What? What just happened?!" asked Odion. He seemed to be freaking out a little bit.

"Gimme a minute!" panted Tobias. He stood, shaking. Teleportation didn't usually take this much out of him, but in this instance, he had teleported not only a couple hundred miles away (a feat he could've, and had done, quite easily) but also had to contend with the enchantments that the Arcane Rebellion had put around that warehouse to prevent such a thing from happening. It was dangerous– exceptionally dangerous–to try and teleport out of a place with protection around it. It was far easier to teleport out of a place like that than to try and teleport into a place with the protection, but even so. Putting all that aside, he had also teleported both himself and Odion. Odion was capable of teleportation, but at that moment, he hadn't been expecting it, so he hadn't lent his strength to Tobias in any capacity.

Odion realized what had happened. He knelt down

beside Tobias and hugged him. In a matter of seconds, Tobias felt his energy come back, recharged and ready to go.

"How did you..?" began Tobias.

"It was the first thing Aurora told me," said Odion sheepishly. "Feeling loved and appreciated is how we perform our magic. We can't do it without feeling accepted, loved, valued. Physical touch and intimacy is the best way to do that. Hugs."

They let go of each other, then Tobias slid down and sat on the ground. Odion sat down next to him; it was rather reminiscent of when Foxton and Finnian had sat down in this same clearing after their school had burned down.

"So, what happened, Toby?"

Tobias didn't say anything. He was thinking back...the worker named Bill had said their names on the loudspeaker. Tobias wasn't a very common name, and he was sure Hunter would've heard it. *So Hunter knows I was there somewhere...*

"Er...Tobias?"

Tobias jumped a little bit and looked at Odion.

"Oh, sorry, Odion. I was lost in thought."

"I see that. So what happened?"

"Didn't you hear our names on the loudspeaker?"

"Yeah."

"We had to get out of there. If Hunter recognized my name…"

Then he looked at Odion, and frowned.

"They said your name too."

"They did."

"So you may be in danger."

"How is that different from how it was before our little adventure?"

Tobias sighed. "I suppose you have a point. Come on. Let's get back to the cottage."

Odion jumped up quickly, but Tobias took a little longer. Odion ended up reaching out a hand and pulling him up after a minute or two.

"Thanks," said Tobias quietly.

The two men slowly walked back to the cottage. Tobias rather thought Odion was being protective of him. He was simultaneously annoyed and amused by this. He had grown fond of Odion, even though they didn't always see eye to eye.

"Toby," said Odion suddenly after a few minutes' walk. "We left the car, and our supplies back there–"

"They'll have to wait. Did you have anything of extreme importance?"

"I suppose not. Just some clothes and stuff. My favorite dress shoes."

"I promise we'll get you some new ones."

"But won't Aurora be mad? Rental cars aren't cheap." "No. We planned to pay for the rental car outright." "How are we going to pay for all that?"

Tobias grimaced. He had hoped to avoid this particular question.

"Ask Aurora."

"Oh, I will."

By the time they reached the edge of the forest, it was early evening. Tobias frowned; he thought he heard some noise in the distance. He turned to the cottage, and saw the source at once. The group of students he had saved– Foxton, Finnian, Lyra, Elena, and Darian–were outside of Aurora's cottage. They seemed to be learning how to channel their magic. He grabbed Odion's arm and told him to wait a moment to watch the proceedings.

"To access your magic, it's imperative that you feel your emotions," Aurora was explaining to the group. "You cannot perform magic if you don't feel it with your heart and soul. You need to be one with it."

"That literally doesn't make any sense," Lyra retorted.

"Perhaps not now, but it will soon enough," Aurora replied calmly. She took a small plastic bag out of her pocket; it was full of sunflower seeds. Sunflowers were easy enough to grow by hand, and even easier to grow by magic.

"Think for a moment about how much you'd like to see this sunflower grow. How beautiful it would be to experience that first-hand; how much it would satisfy you to have a fully grown sunflower in your hand right now."

She turned to Finnian and said gently, "Wouldn't you love to experience that, Finnian? The feeling of growing something with your emotion?"

"Er...I guess," Finnian stammered shyly.

"That's all magic is, really. You are channeling your emotions, your feelings. You're channeling this into energy that flows through you. These sunflowers—" she grabbed three seeds from her bag, placed them into her open palm on her other hand, and three huge sunflowers bloomed almost instantly, "--are just the beginning."

"But isn't magic supposed to be a weapon?" asked Elena rather rudely. "What good's a sunflower in a fight if we're fighting against fire?"

Instantly, one of the sunflowers in Aurora's hand leaped out of her hand and around Elena's neck. Seemingly of its own accord, it squeezed tightly around her neck. Elena gasped. Lyra screamed and tried to pull the sunflower off of her. But it wouldn't budge; Lyra's pulling on it just made it squeeze even tighter. Darian screamed at Aurora, "Stop it! Don't you see you made your point?!"

Elena was starting to turn blue; she couldn't breathe. Tobias glanced over at Odion, who was very white and pale. He had obviously never seen Aurora like this. Tobias sighed. He loved Aurora very much, but this was a side of her he was less than fond of. And unfortunately, it seemed to happen rather often. Someone would insult her, or her skills with magic, and she would step well over a line to prove her point.

The sunflower released its grip on Elena. She choked as she gasped for breath, tears streaming down her face. Lyra was sobbing quietly into her sister's shoulder, hugging her tightly. Darian looked pale and furious. Foxton and Finnian both looked nervous and uncomfortable.

"I think that," said Aurora firmly, "will conclude our lesson for today. Please mind what insults you give me and my plants in the future."

With that, she strode over to the cottage door and slammed it shut.

Odion made to run over to the students, but Tobias held him back once again.

"Wait," he whispered. "I want to see their reaction."

The girls continued to cry quietly. Elena had regained her breath but was obviously still shaken. Darian was pacing around the group, outraged.

"She could've killed you! As if we haven't lost enough already! Now, we are being attacked by these freaks! Why can't we just go home?! Why did that creep, Mr. Thornfield, bring us here in the first place?!"

Tobias' heart sank. He wasn't really sure what he had been expecting, but to hear the anger and resentment in Darian's words was devastating to him. He sank a little bit, grabbing a nearby tree trunk for support.

After a few more minutes, Foxton timidly suggested they return to their safe house. The group agreed, the girls rather reluctantly. Tobias saw the group glance up the road, the freeway leading away from the cottage and from Bellwater. That was a stretch of road that went on for miles before seeing the next town; they would never make it on foot. Of course, Tobias knew that, but he wasn't sure the young adults did. After a brief, whispered conversation that Tobias couldn't hear, the group, led by Foxton, walked back down the hill.

Once the group was out of sight, Odion turned to Tobias. He looked furious.

"I want to go have a word with Aurora. That was totally uncalled for!"

"Listen, Odion! I agree. But Aurora is not to be messed with. Her word is law around here."

Odion looked at Tobias with shock and unmistakably hurt.

"You're defending her?"

"I'm not defending her actions," Tobias replied quickly. "Just…don't go picking a fight with Aurora! It's not gonna do any of us any good."

Odion swore and turned away from Tobias. He paced around the patch of trees in a manner similar to what Darian had done a few minutes ago. He was silent for a few minutes; Tobias thought he knew what was coming. Then–

"Listen, Toby! Do you need me to go in there with you? I don't think I can face her right now."

Tobias had been expecting this. "No, you can go home if you'd like," he replied.

Odion nodded. "Alright. Good night, Toby!"

He teleported away.

Tobias stumbled his way up to the cottage door. He knocked and entered. Aurora was sitting at the kitchen table, helping herself to a brownie and drinking a cup of coffee.

"Toby! You're back already?!"

"Yeah, Aurora. I have good news!"

He pulled out his cellphone and put it down on the kitchen table. Aurora beamed at him. "You hacked their computer system? Nice job! And you did it in one day, too!"

Aurora snatched up the phone and opened it up. She

knew his passcode, of course; they were, after all, best friends.

"Let's take a look at some of these! Shall we?"

One by one, they opened all of the files that Tobias had copied from the Arcane Rebellion's computer to his cellphone. There was little of anything important; cruise ship schedules, financial documents (the Arcane Rebellion was making a killing with their cruises), and business plans. This made sense, given that the computer had been in the basement of the warehouse for their cruise ship.

Then, there was only one document left. Aurora opened it hurriedly and frowned. Tobias looked over her shoulder.

There was a complete profile of all of the teachers and students at Bellwater Academy. They had everything: names, dates of birth, social security numbers, magic specializations, resumes, an estimated "power level" that they had undoubtedly come up with on their own (Tobias was happy to see he had the highest power level of them all), even their favorite colors and the names of their second-grade teachers. After making a mental note to change his passwords, Tobias turned to Aurora and said, "This isn't good."

"Yeah, no kidding. How the hell did they get this?"

"Could they have hacked the school's system?"

"The school doesn't have all this information."

"It has some of it."

"Sure, but not this much, Toby."

Tobias thought for a minute. Then he asked, "Who would have access to this information? You?" "No.

I don't know this much about our staff."

"Percival Ion?"

"We've been over this, Toby."

"I know, but we haven't really ruled him out." "He

doesn't know about us," said Aurora firmly.

Tobias sighed and decided that, while that was concerning, there were bigger concerns for them at the moment.

"Aurora," said Tobias quickly. "I just remembered…Hunter had mentioned an attack on Bellwater."

"What?!" asked Aurora sharply. "When?"

"When we were in the basement, we overheard him talking to this guy named Ted."

"No, when is the attack going to take place?"

"I don't know. They were still trying to figure out the details."

Aurora sighed. "I wish this had been the first thing you told me." She rubbed her head, then looked around.

"Hey…where is Odion, by the way?"

"He…er…we kind of saw your lesson with the students, and he was pretty upset about it."

"Oh?"

"Yeah. Aurora, you did go a little crazy with the sunflower thing."

"She was disrespectful, Toby. I would expect you to understand."

"Yes, but all the same, Aurora. She's a teenage girl who just lost her family and friends. Maybe a little grace and compassion would go a long way."

"If I didn't know better, I'd say Percival was rubbing off on you."

"You take that back."

Tobias threw a brownie at her. Aurora caught it easily and threw it into her open mouth, smiling.

"Yeah, you're probably right, Toby. You always are. I'll follow up with her tomorrow."

"Make sure Odion sees you doing that too. He wasn't happy with you."

"He won't be at school tomorrow. Remember? We got him a long-term sub."

"Oh yes, the long-term sub you couldn't get for Agatha

for some reason. So you got me fired instead." "The very same."

"Ok, but what are we going to do about this Arcane Rebellion attack on Bellwater?"

"Prepare for it! That's all we can do, Toby. We don't know when it's happening. Just that it is."

Tobias nodded, then stood up and stretched.

"Well, I think I'm gonna hit the hay. I'm exhausted."

She waved at him, bidding him goodnight. He walked to her guest bedroom and flopped onto the bed, still in his deckhand uniform from earlier, and fell asleep almost at once.

Chapter Twelve:
Best of Friends, Best of Enemies

Aurora woke Tobias up early the next morning. She was standing over him, opening the curtains and gesturing for him to get up.

"What's the matter?" He asked groggily, rubbing his eyes and yawning.

"I need you to be awake in case we need you," said Aurora briskly.

"Need me? For what? I'm not teaching."

"You're not teaching at Bellwater. But I'm having you teach my class tonight. I think…" she sighed, "I think it would be best for me to take the night off from teaching the new students."

"You want me to teach them earth magic? I don't know anything about that element, Aurora," retorted Tobias, stifling a yawn.

"Teach them wind or lightning then, Toby! I just don't think it's a good idea for me to teach them right now."

He picked up his phone off the bedside table to check the time. "So you wake me up at six a.m. to tell me I'm teaching your class at six p.m.? You couldn't have texted me this afternoon?" he asked, rather annoyed with her.

"Nope. Like I said, I need you awake. If they attack the school today, I want to be ready."

But the attack didn't come. Aurora left for school thirty minutes later, wearing a black dress and high heels, while Tobias sat in the cottage, keeping an eye on the television and occasionally peeking outside. It was a cloudy day with light rain drizzling down from the sky; it was Tobias' favorite kind of day. The weather provided the perfect excuse to curl up with a good book and isolate himself under a warm blanket.

At five o'clock, the cottage door opened, and Aurora stepped inside. Tobias quickly stood up; he had been dozing lazily in an armchair. His book had fallen out of his lap and onto the floor.

"How was work, Aurora?" he asked hurriedly, picking the book up off the floor before she noticed.

"Oh, it was fine."

"Did you apologize to those kids?"

Aurora looked sheepishly down at the floor.

"Aurora!" he said sternly.

"I didn't get a chance to, Toby. Percival came into my office and gave me about a dozen tasks to complete by the end of the day."

Tobias sighed. Typical Percival, he thought dully.

"Alright, you'll just have to do it tonight then. Where will the class take place?"

"Right outside the cottage, where it was last night."

"Did you talk to Odion today?" he questioned.

Aurora turned away from Tobias. Not making eye contact, she muttered, "We might have run into each other."

"Did he say anything?"

"No, but his body language said it all. He's mad at me."

"Well, you were a bit harsh…"

"Yes, I know, Toby. Didn't I already explain that I'm sorry?"

"To me, you did. Not to them."

Aurora grabbed a nearby potholder and threw it at Tobias. Tobias caught it, frowning. "I'm serious, Aurora. You really do owe them an apology."

"Yes, I'm aware. I will apologize to them tonight."

After a quick dinner of grilled cheese sandwiches, Tobias and Aurora went outside and waited for the students to arrive. Just after six o'clock, Foxton and Finnian were seen walking up the hill towards the cottage.

"Late as usual, gentlemen," said Tobias sternly. "Sorry,

Mr. T—er, Tobias," said Finnian timidly.

Tobias looked around, frowning. "Where are the others?"

The two boys also frowned. "They didn't tell you? They told us they weren't coming tonight. They apparently had another meeting."

"Another meeting? With whom?"

"They didn't say. They just said they had another meeting."

"They said they cleared it with Aurora," Foxton chimed in.

Tobias turned to Aurora. "I presume they didn't clear it with you?"

"Nope. They sure didn't."

"I'm gonna go look for them, Aurora."

Aurora nodded. "I'll teach these two a few things while you're gone."

"No strangulation, please!" Tobias yelled sarcastically as he jogged down the hill towards the village of Bellwater.

Aurora made a rude hand gesture at him, then turned to the two boys and began explaining the intricacies of growing vegetables from seeds—very similar to growing flowers, but you had to feel an extra strong sense of belonging.

The hill was not big; it took Tobias less than five minutes to reach the village. Small houses were on either side of the Main Street. Most of these were occupied by non-magic users, though a few were their own spellcasters. Tobias hoped they wouldn't have this meeting in a random house, and had almost resigned himself to the fact that he would have to start randomly knocking on doors. Then he remembered his excursion into the Arcane Rebellion warehouse yesterday and had a better idea.

A power line was feet from him. He grabbed it, embracing the pole in a giant bear hug. Instantly, using the electricity from the power lines, he could see into each of the houses and buildings of the village.

A woman changing a baby's diaper. A man cursing loudly at his video game. An old married couple bickering over the dinner table. A young couple making out. Not one of these houses had any sign of Lyra, Elena, or Darian.

Tobias frowned. Something was odd.

He began not running but walking briskly down Main Street towards the police station on the other end of town. He wasn't really sure what he was looking for, but there was a weird vibe in the neighborhood. He hadn't spent a ton of time in the village of Bellwater before, but he knew enough to recognize when something major was about to go down.

Then, he spotted them. There they were: Lyra, Elena, and Darian. But there was a fourth figure with them. They were down an alleyway between the bar and a coffee shop. Tobias thought it would be an ideal place to stage a meeting without witnesses.

"There you are!" He cried as he approached. None of the figures turned toward him. He frowned and moved closer.

The figures instantly lit ablaze with flames and rushed toward Tobias. He managed to avoid their fiery attacks by snapping his fingers towards the power line, which was directly overhead. Electricity from the powerline stopped the fire in its tracks, but there was a loud laugh.

Tobias turned, expecting to see Hunter. He was correct; his old friend was standing there, flames in his hands, ready for battle.

But he wasn't alone.

Percival Ion was standing next to Hunter, clutching a rifle that was pointing directly at Tobias.

"Well, well!" He said smugly. "I knew it'd be you."

"Percival!" spat Tobias, "What are you doing here? Hunter, what are you playing at? Where are the kids?"

"They aren't here, Toby. Your dear…friend," he purred the word, "saw to that. Strangling a student with a sunflower? Has Aurora completely lost it? They reported her directly to Principal Ion," he nodded towards Percival, "and he had concerns. You see, he's been working with us the last few months, trying to get rid of your meddlesome friends."

Tobias glared at them both. He had been right all along. It was Percival Ion who was working with the Arcane Rebellion.

"He reached out to us, and asked for our assistance. We were glad to provide it. Dear Elena, Lyra, and Darian have been taken away from here. Oh, thank you!" he added as an afterthought, "For resurrecting Darian. That was most useful, Tobias."

Tobias clenched his fists. He was so angry with Hunter right now. "Hunt," he asked, forcing himself to stay calm, "Why are you doing this?"

"What, did you think I was gonna let that bitch Aurora bully me forever, Tobias? No, sir! You may allow her to walk all over you, but I, for one, will not. The Arcane Rebellion is where our loyalties should lay."

"But Hunter, think of everything Aurora has done for you! For us!"

"Like what?"

"Like teaching us magic, for starters! We wouldn't be nearly as powerful as we are now without the support of Aurora!" he defended her angrily. He knew Aurora wasn't always in the right, but she had done so much for them; it hurt him to hear Hunter say those words about her.

"You don't know that, Tobias. You don't know what we are capable of. With or without her, we got to where we are, and we've proven our abilities!"

"Hunter!" Tobias was practically pleading with his old friend, "Please, Hunter! Don't do this! Come home—"

Percival pulled the trigger on his rifle. The bullet went blasting towards Tobias and missed him by inches. The blast from the gun made both Tobias and Hunter jump backward; Hunter landed gracefully on his feet and shot a ball of fire directly at Tobias.

Tobias landed clumsily; he tripped over his own feet, then fell on his butt on the hard ground. The fireball soared over the top of his head, and exploded into the alleyway, igniting everything in the vicinity on fire. Tobias teleported directly behind Percival Ion. But Percival had been expecting this, as though he had been forewarned about Tobias' ability to teleport; he turned around before Tobias had even reached his destination.

Percival pulled the trigger again. This time, the bullet hit Tobias squarely in the chest. Tobias gasped, then grabbed his chest, where a dark red strain started to show on his shirt.

Someone screamed. Tobias saw Hunter launch a second fireball, not at Tobias, but at Percival Ion, who was hit directly in the face with the ball of flames. Percival was blasted backward, screaming and flailing through the air. Then he slammed into the wall of the coffee shop and moved no more. Hunter ran over to Tobias, jumping over rubble as he past, and held Tobias in his arms.

Then, out of nowhere, several people teleported into

the alleyway.

"Hunter!" Hunter recognized that voice; it was Aurora. "What have you done, Hunter? Put him down this instant!"

"You!" Hunter spat at her. Before he could say anything else, however, a jet of white light hit him square in the back. Hunter turned around, and from his arms, Tobias saw Sabrina Braithwaite and Lucien Rodgson facing him.

"Anti-Teleportation Spell," Sabrina said coldly. "You're not going anywhere, Hunter. You're surrounded. Put. Him. Down!"

Just like the name implies, an Anti-Teleportation Spell would prevent a spellcaster from using teleportation magic. The effect was usually temporary; how long it would last was dependent on the strength of both the spellcaster using the spell and the person against whom it was used. In this case, Sabrina—a formidable mage in her own right—had used the spell on Hunter—also a formidable mage—so it would likely last an hour at most.

"Toby!"

It was Odion. He had teleported onto the scene a minute later than everyone else; he ran up to him and looked at his chest wound.

"We need to get him to the hospital!"

"Get away from him!" Hunter snarled, pulling Tobias closer to him. "I don't recognize you. Who are you?"

"I'm Odion," he retorted snappishly, "and if we don't get Toby to a doctor soon—"

"I will take him. How dare you call him Toby! You get out of here!"

"Hunter, do you actually believe we are going to allow you to walk out of here?" Aurora snapped.

"Hunt!" Tobias gasped weakly. Hunter looked at him with concern in his eyes.

"What is it, Toby?"

"Let me go with…with Odion." Tobias gasped weakly, as though every word was costing him dearly.

Hunter froze. It was obvious he hadn't expected this; Tobias, his oldest and dearest friend, chose someone else over him.

"Toby. You don't even know him—"

"Yes, I do," said Tobias proudly. "He…he's been good to me the last few days. You, on the other hand—" Tobias looked sadly at his old friend, "--I haven't seen you in months. No word, no call, nothing."

Hunter didn't say anything. His fists clenched in the air a few times. Tobias peeled himself out of Hunter's arms; he knew Hunter wouldn't do anything to him now. Hunter allowed him to go. Whether it was due to shock, not wanting to hurt Tobias further, or a combination of the two, Hunter did nothing to stop his old friend. Odion went and grabbed Tobias; he held him up while Tobias put an arm around Odion. Together, they teleported away.

Hunter turned around. Directly in front of him was Aurora. To his right was Matilda Carrington. Behind him, he knew, were Sabrina and Lucien. Agatha O'Connor was to his left; the old woman was leaning heavily on a cane, but still was standing upright and seemed ready for a fight. He knew he was outmatched. With a sigh, he said to the group at large:

"All right. What do you want from me?"

Aurora snapped her fingers. Vines appeared out of thin air and wrapped themselves tightly around Hunter. They didn't get around his neck, but they did secure his arms and legs. He couldn't move; the effort made him fall over.

"Come on!" said Aurora curtly. "We are going back to the cottage."

With surprising strength, Aurora picked him up with a fireman's lift and carried him back to the cottage. Sabrina, Lucien, and Matilda followed close behind. As Sabrina had cast an Anti-Teleportation Spell on Hunter, they couldn't teleport him away; they had to walk there the old-fashioned way. Once the group was adequately far away, Agatha teleported away; she would not be up to transporting Hunter up the hill.

They had barely reached Main Street when at least a dozen police cars showed up. Lights flashing, sirens blazing, they pulled up and surrounded the group. The police exited their cars and pulled out their firearms, pointing them at the group who were seemingly kidnapping Hunter.

One of the officers—seemingly the one in charge— pulled out a megaphone and began talking to Aurora.

"Put the man down and come quietly! We have you surrounded."

Aurora swore and looked around at Sabrina, Lucien, and Matilda. The three of them looked unsure. Hunter, meanwhile, started crying out, "Please, please, officers! Help me!" Aurora slapped his vines, and they instantly wrapped themselves around Hunter's mouth. She was furious with herself; how could they have let this happen? This was obviously Hunter's plan all along: it put them in a situation where their only way out was through brute force.

But taking out the entire police force of Bellwater was, in her opinion, a huge mistake. Absolutely nothing good could come of that. She had no doubt in her mind that her group absolutely *could* overpower the police officers in front of them. Quite frankly, she could probably do it single-handedly. However, that would not go unnoticed, and they would need to immediately leave Bellwater, never to return. Questions would be asked, and it would be a huge mess. Unfortunately, none of the group had thought to wear face masks or anything either, so if they didn't get rid of these officers, they would undoubtedly get sketches of their group and eventually be tracked down.

With that in mind, she knew there was only one thing to do.

She flicked her wrist, and the ground in front of the police cars trembled. The officers yelled; some of them fired their weapons at the group of magicians, but Lucien held out his hand, and the bullets blew back toward the officers with a powerful gust of wind. They struck their owners down. The force of the quake caused the police cars to overturn and go flying, smashing into several of the officers. The ground in front of them was now filled with broken car parts, blood, and torn limbs from the fallen police officers.

"Aurora!" whispered Sabrina frantically, "What have we done?"

Chapter Thirteen:
Change in Leadership

Tobias and Odion appeared directly in front of the hospital, about a thousand yards away from the alleyway where Tobias had gotten shot. The hospital was in a nearby town directly south of Bellwater Academy. Tobias was clutching the bullet wound with his hand, trying to stem the bleeding. Odion was helping support him; Tobias relied heavily on Odion to help him walk. It took them a minute to walk through the front doors, but once they did, they were immediately greeted by nurses who, seeing the blood stain on Tobias' shirt, rushed him into the emergency room and left Odion in the waiting room, covered in Tobias' blood.

Odion sighed and sat down in an unoccupied chair. The waiting room was small; only a few chairs and tables with outdated magazines sat around the room. A television was playing cartoons in the corner, right next to some old toys and figures that young children could play with while they waited for the doctors.

Mindlessly, Odion grabbed one of the magazines and flipped through it. It was boring, useless information about celebrities who were cheating on each other, epic weight loss programs, or other scams that people occupied their time with for some reason. Odion quickly put it down and grabbed another one, this one containing several recipes for sourdough bread and other homemade treats. Odion wasn't much of a baker, so he put that one down as well. The third magazine he took was all about sports. Odion was an athlete, but reading about sports and athletes was quite different from actually playing them.

"Sir?"

Odion blinked in surprise; there was a young woman sitting at the registration desk. She beckoned Odion over.

"Are you with the man who was just brought in?" "Yes."

"Are you next of kin?"

"Er–no."

"Do you have a way to contact his next of kin?"

"No, not really."

"What is his name?"

"Tobias Thornfield."

"His date of birth?"

"Um…I'm not sure."

"Are the two of you close?"

"We're friends, but not medical proxies, kind of thing?"

"I see. Forgive me. I just assumed…"

Her voice trailed away. Then, she quickly turned away from Odion, blushing profusely. Odion rolled his eyes and went back to the waiting room.

He sat for over an hour, filled with anxiety about Tobias. He flipped through the magazines a few more times, examined what was going on with the television, and even went and tried to speak to the registration nurse again, but she wasn't there. At one point, he thought he felt something resembling a tremor on the ground, but it quickly disappeared, so Odion thought nothing of it.

He thought of Tobias. Was he going to be okay? He had lost a lot of blood. But, he was coherent when he had been brought in. He knew Tobias was in the best place for him.

He also thought of that Hunter character. He was very unsure what to make of him; it was obvious that he cared deeply for Tobias, but he had also gotten him shot. Odion frowned as he considered this. He hadn't seen any kind of gun or weapon on Hunter's person, though it was also true that he had been more focused on getting Tobias out of harm's way than anything else. He was sure Aurora and the others would find it.

Odion had heard the sound of a gunshot just outside his front door; he lived not too far from the coffee shop where the alley was and was just entering his house when he heard it. One of the first things he had learned from Aurora was the ability to communicate with other mages telepathically. You had to concentrate hard on who you wanted to communicate with, and then you could have short conversations with that person as long as they were relatively close.

Aurora, he had thought with all his might.

Odion? What is it?

I heard a gunshot down here. What?

I heard a gunshot not too far from my house. In

Bellwater? Tobias just ran down there.

He did? Why?

We...seem to be missing a few students.

What do you mean?

There's no time to explain. I will gather the others, and we will investigate this. Wait for my signal.

He had waited for merely thirty seconds or so before Aurora contacted him again.

Odion!

Yes, Aurora? Did you find something?

Tobias is in an alleyway not too far from your house between the bar and the coffee shop. We are all meeting there in about ten seconds.

He teleported to that location about thirty seconds later; he had been in the middle of changing his clothes when Aurora had initially contacted him. And that's when he saw Tobias...

A nurse walked out to the waiting room. Odion stood up quickly; he was the only one in the waiting room. Surely, they would have news for him at this point?

The nurse looked at him and asked, "Are you here for Tobias Thornfield?"

"Yes, ma'am."

"He is in surgery right now. The doctor is optimistic about his chances; he lost a lot of blood, but after a nice, long recovery period, he should be fine."

Odion smiled at her. "Thank you, miss!" He said politely. "When can I see him?"

"Tomorrow. You should–" she looked him up and down, "--go home and get some rest yourself. Looks like you need it."

He nodded at her, thanked her again, and turned to leave. The nurse walked back into the emergency room. He had barely taken a step out of the door when–

Odion!

Aurora! What's happening? Did you get that Hunter guy?

Yes, but there's a problem. I need you to come to the

cottage at once.

Without a second thought, he teleported to the cottage. He walked right inside the front door, and was instantly greeted by the sight of Sabrina, Lucien, Matilda, and Aurora gathered around the dining room table. They seemed to be having an intense conversation. Sabrina was talking:

"I understand you felt it was the right thing to do, Aurora, but all those innocent people lost their lives because of us! Surely you can appreciate that? Not to mention, at some point, people are going to notice that half of their police force is lying dead in the middle of the town!"

Odion blinked. "I beg your pardon?" he asked Sabrina politely.

"Our dear…leader," said Lucien sarcastically, indicating Aurora, "decided it'd be a good idea to stage a massive police massacre in the middle of town."

Aurora glared at him.

"We were surrounded, with guns drawn at us, in case you'd forgotten! What would you have done in that situation?"

"I would have surrendered!" roared Lucien; he was livid. "I would have told the police that we stopped a madman from killing our friend!"

"And how would you have explained the sudden disappearance of this friend?"

"I would simply say that he was already at the hospital thanks to our actions! This can easily be verified. He is in the hospital, I take it?" he questioned Odion, a sudden look of concern in his eyes.

The group turned to Odion. "Oh my goodness!" whispered Sabrina. "We didn't even ask–how is he?"

"The doctors expect a full recovery," Odion said quickly. "He's in surgery, and we can see him tomorrow. Tell me more about this massacre!"

"I would hardly call it a massacre," Aurora replied sharply. "It was self-defense! We need to protect ourselves–"

"That was not self-defense, Aurora," Matilda retorted calmly. "That was an attack–an unprovoked attack on innocent human lives." She spoke as though she found the entire situation nothing more than an amusement, quite the opposite of Sabrina and Lucien.

"They were pointing their guns at us!" roared Aurora. "And they fired if you recall! Because you–" she pointed at Lucien accusingly, "--used magic to kill half of them with their own bullets!"

"They only shot at us because you caused an earthquake to assault them!" Lucien snapped back at her. "Like I said, if we had just surrendered, we could–"

"Where is Hunter?" asked Odion suddenly.

"He's in the living room," said Sabrina quickly. It was obvious she wanted the yelling to stop. Odion stepped into the living room. However, there was no sign of Hunter.

"Er—are you guys sure?"

The mages jumped up from the dining room table and raced into the living room.

"What? Where did he go?" asked Matilda, looking around for a sign of the man.

"He couldn't have teleported! My spell should prevent him from doing that," Sabrina cried, sounding panicked.

"And my vines should have prevented him from moving an inch," Aurora said quietly.

"Didn't Hunter specialize in fire magic?" asked Odion.

"Yes, he did. But he couldn't have melted those vines. Unless…"

Aurora gasped. The window in the living room was wide open. He had an accomplice."

"An accomplice? Who?"

"Was there anyone else at the warehouse with him when you and Tobias investigated?" asked Aurora quickly.

"Er—yeah, there was this guy named Ted who was walking with him—"

Aurora swore. "He had help," she said sheepishly.

"This is my fault. I should have known better than to keep the window open."

"You're really on a roll today, Aurora. First, the police massacre, then the person who actually started all of this gets away because of your negligence?" Matilda questioned quietly. The others muttered in agreement.

Aurora's heart sank. She hadn't expected this; the others seemed to turn on her quickly.

"We need to come up with a plan," said Sabrina sharply. She seemed to be taking charge, Aurora noted. "Police reinforcements will be arriving here any second. Perhaps even the National Guard, if they are concerned enough and word of this reaches the right people."

"What do you propose we do?"

"Go into hiding!" she said quickly. "We can cast apparitions of ourselves with our magic to conduct our day-to-day business for the time being. If the police question the apparitions, we'll know they are looking for us. It will look too suspicious if we all immediately go into hiding with no rhyme or reason. At least if the apparitions are still out and about, that will allow us to still conduct our normal lives."

Casting an apparition was to project an image of yourself or another person. The apparitions could walk and talk; they had all the appearance of a "normal" individual. The caster could make the apparitions disappear at a moment's notice. It was relatively easy to cast these apparitions, but you did have to maintain a certain degree of proximity to the location where the apparitions were. A spellcaster couldn't project an apparition more than maybe a hundred miles away from their current location.

"And where will we actually hide while we use these projections?" asked Lucien.

"The forest clearing?" suggested Odion. "No one ever goes in there except Toby and I."

Aurora and Sabrina both nodded. "That's a good idea," They said together.

"It will at least give us something to go on," admitted Lucien. "If the police officers are dead, they can't exactly identify us. We'll have a better idea as to what to do after we have a clearer picture of what the public and the police think happened. Maybe they'll think it was an explosion or an actual earthquake or something."

"In the meantime," suggested Matilda, "we should probably keep an eye on the news and media coverage. Check the social media pages, too! Make sure we know what the word on the street is!"

"Odion, can you be in charge of that?" asked Sabrina kindly. Odion nodded.

"Great! Well, I suggest we retire to the clearing for the evening. Tomorrow will come early. We can send apparitions to check on Tobias in the morning."

Chapter Fourteen:
Orders

Two men—a strong, young man of Mexican descent, and a chubby, squat man—teleported into a large room. It was extremely dark in the room; it had no windows or doors and could only be entered through teleportation. The only source of light came from lights that hung on the wall. These lights, Hunter knew, were powered by magic.

A bulky table was in the middle of the room, with a large space filled with water in the middle. Hunter knew that space was used for scrying. Around a dozen people were already seated around the table. Hunter recognized several of these faces; they were all members of the Arcane Rebellion. He nodded at each one in turn as he went to take his seat. There were two empty chairs: one at the head of the table, and the other to the immediate right of the head. Hunter sat to the left of the head of the table. Ted sat somewhere in the middle.

After a few minutes, two more figures appeared in the room, smiling at the crowd assembled before them. The woman—a tall, beautiful blonde woman wearing an elegant red dress and lipstick, took her seat at the head of the table. The man, chubby and middle-aged, sat to her immediate right.

"Madame Braithwaite," the crowd greeted her

cheerily. "Lucien."

"Hello, everyone," Sabrina Braithwaite called out to the crowd assembled around her. "We have updates for all of you," she said, smiling widely. "Hunter, your performance was marvelous! Just what we needed to undermine Aurora in front of the students and the other members of the Bellwater Mages."

"It was Lucien's idea to get the police involved," Hunter added, with a grin towards Lucien. "That was fantastic! How'd you know she'd attack them like that?"

"I didn't," Lucien admitted. "I actually planned for her to get arrested. But this works out too. Matilda and Agatha are…concerned. As is young Odion. I'm sure the other apprentices they have, as well as their other agents working throughout the country, will soon see the error of their ways and join us."

Hunter nodded. "And of Tobias?"

There was silence around the group for a minute.

"We…are unsure at this time," said Sabrina politely, but firmly. "I think it is unwise to allow him and Aurora to communicate with each other. Hunter, please make no mistake: we did not intend for Percival Ion to shoot your friend. You have our deepest condolences."

Hunter didn't say anything; he stared blankly into space for a minute, then said, "I killed the bastard."

"As I would have done," said Lucien reassuringly. "You don't need to worry about that. We will excuse the penalty for attacking one of our own in this instance. Percival—while not a mage—was working on contract for us in this instance, as you know."

"But we do need to talk about Tobias, Hunter," said Sabrina. "He killed Avery. I know he thought he was doing the right thing–and I know he did bring us these excellent new disciples," she waved her hand at the pool of water, and three figures–sleeping in a comfortable cabin–appeared in front of them: two twin teenage girls and a young man with blond hair, "but he cannot be allowed to get away with murdering one of us."

Hunter gulped. He thought he knew what was coming, and his suspicions were confirmed a minute later:

"You need to kill him."

"I can't," he whispered. "Please…anyone else–"

"No, Hunter. It needs to be you."

"But why can't someone else do it?"

"We need to test your strength," said Lucien, watching Hunter carefully. "And your resolve. How devoted are you to us? Or are your loyalties still with him and the Bellwater mages?"

"With them?" asked Hunter incredulously.

"Your loyalty to Aurora is undoubtedly all but erased. Your loyalty to Tobias is in question here. Being loyal to Tobias means being disloyal to us. So, can you do it? Can you follow our orders and do what needs to be done?"

Hunter said nothing for several seconds, then said,

"When do I need to have it done?"

"Do it soon, Hunter. Aurora will put him to work undermining us as soon as he gets out of that hospital. She has put herself in a vulnerable position. Having her commit that police massacre, while not exactly as planned, was brilliant for getting the other teachers to question her methods. But Tobias, he has unwavering loyalty to her, I'm afraid."

"Not unwavering," said Hunter quickly. "He's questioned her before."

"But he's never actually moved against her in any meaningful way," Lucien countered. "His actions are always to advance her agenda."

"But couldn't…couldn't we let him join us?"

There were laughs and gasps around the table at this. Several of the people sneered at Hunter. Ted—the chubby, middle-aged man who had teleported into the room with Hunter, exclaimed, "He's a murderer, Hunter! Think of poor Avery. How much of a slap in the face would it be to let him join us after that?!"

Hunter sat in silence. He knew arguing was no good, that it had come to this. Tobias' actions had proven where his loyalty lay. And now he, Hunter, needed to prove his loyalty to the Arcane Rebellion. For his actions hadn't always been about the Arcane Rebellion, or its advancement, or its protection. He knew it, the others knew it, and Sabrina and Lucien certainly knew it.

"With Tobias out of the way, it is only a matter of time before the others join us!" Sabrina was almost giddy with excitement. "Aurora will fall, Matilda and Agatha and all their apprentices will either be slain or will join us, and we will have complete control over magic once more!"

The crowd cheered loudly at her words. Lucien stood up, embraced her tightly, and kissed her on the lips. Power seemed to flow between the two; their love and connection was stronger than any other magic in the room. They would soon be an unstoppable force, Hunter thought dully. He did not participate in the celebrations; he was too busy thinking about what his loyalty to the Rebellion was going to cost him.

Chapter Fifteen: Recovery

Tobias woke up in discomfort. Not pain per se, but he could feel that something had happened to his lower body. It took a minute for him to register the events that had transpired when he had last been conscious.

I got shot, he thought to himself, grimacing. Percival Ion had shot him. Of course he had. And Hunter was with him.

Tobias moved to stand up, but he quickly abandoned the idea. While he was lying down, there was a mild level of discomfort, but as soon as he started moving around, that discomfort quickly turned to pain. So, he simply lay in the bed and surveyed his surroundings.

He was in a hospital room. The walls were painted pure white; there was nothing in the room except for a chair and a small television set. The door to his room was closed. It didn't look like anyone had been in there recently to check on him. He noticed that he was hooked up to an IV; he had no medical knowledge, so naturally, he didn't know what this was, but he assumed it was for pain. Getting shot didn't feel so good.

He noticed there was a remote on his leg. Grabbing it, he called for a nurse. A middle-aged woman came in a few minutes later.

"You're awake," she said, not unkindly but also rather quickly; she seemed to be in something of a hurry. She took a look at his IV. "Looks good there," she said. She was wearing a stethoscope around her neck. She pulled it off and took his heartbeat, then took a quick pulse. "You seem like you're doing well, Mr. Thornfield!"

Tobias smiled weakly at her. "What time is it?" he croaked. He hadn't spoken for a while.

"It is eleven o'clock in the morning. You were nearly unconscious when your friend brought you in three days ago. The surgeon was able to patch you up, and we did a blood transfusion, but you're still going to need to stay in here for a while so we can monitor you."

"Have I had any visitors?"

"Yes, as a matter of fact. Two people came by. I didn't talk to them much. They just asked how you were doing and when we could expect you to wake up."

"Are you surprised that I am awake? Is that a good sign?"

"It's good," she said, smiling at him now. "And you're talking and coherent and everything."

"Did anyone else come in with me?"

"No, I don't believe so."

"The man who shot me?"

"I'm afraid I do not know. The police haven't been in yet. They...they've been busy dealing with a rather unfortunate situation of their own."

"Oh? What happened?"

"An earthquake of some sort, it sounds like. But the whole thing is awfully suspicious. An earthquake? Take out half the police force?"

"An earthquake? Really?"

Making a mental note to ask Aurora about that—he had a sinking feeling she would have some information for him—he proceeded to ask the nurse, "When can I be discharged?"

"Oh, not for a while yet, honey. Like I said, we need to monitor your vitals for a while. You were kind of touch and go there for a little bit, I won't lie. But the surgeon took care of you."

"Okay. Thank you, ma'am."

She gave him one last look before leaving the room, closing the door quietly behind her. Tobias, who had just now realized he was only wearing a hospital gown and slippers, wanted his old clothes back, but he didn't want to call her back again when she had just left. He sighed. They were probably unwearable anyway, now that he thought about it.

He wanted to talk to Aurora. He knew that mages could use telepathy to communicate with one another from a distance, but this was an area of magic that Tobias had never been able to get the hang of. You had to really concentrate on who you wanted to talk to and what you wanted to say. His attention was far too unfocused for that. Plus, he generally preferred to be left alone, and he felt he would be interrupted far more often than was necessary if he did have that ability. Still, it would be nice if he could reach out to his friends and let them know he was awake.

He spent a fair amount of time that afternoon in bed, watching television, sleeping, or thinking about Aurora, Odion, and Hunter. Aurora owed him an explanation about the earthquake. Did she cause that? Hunter owed him an explanation about what Percival Ion was doing working with him, and how he ended up getting shot. And Odion…well, he supposed Odion didn't really owe him anything. But it would have been nice to see him.

He had no visitors—other than the nurse again to check on his vitals, and a small lunch delivered by a hospital assistant—until around 4 p.m. Tobias could tell the time because *The Kelly Clarkson Show* had just started, and he made it a habit to watch it after work each day. However, Kelly had barely finished her Kellyoke of the day when there was a knock on the door, and two figures popped in. Aurora, closely followed by Odion.

"Toby!"

They both ran up to him and hugged him. He tried to hug them back, but couldn't; he noticed that when they hugged, they went right through him. They couldn't actually touch. Which meant they were using apparitions to make this appearance.

"Took you guys long enough. I've been up for a few hours!"

"Yes, yes, never mind that. We've had a busy day."

"Sounds like it. What's this I hear about an *earthquake* attacking police, Aurora?"

Aurora paused from fiddling with Tobias's bedsheets and tucking him in to look at Tobias, frowning. "How did you know?"

"The nurse told me. The police say it was just an earthquake, but I feel like there's more to the story than that."

"There is," Aurora admitted, though Tobias could tell she was rather reluctant to do so. "I'd prefer, however, not to discuss it here."

"Is that why you're using apparitions?"

"Yes, we need to be careful. None of us have been questioned by the police yet, but just as a precaution…"

"Questioned by the police? Are you sure there's nothing I need to know about?"

"I never said there's nothing you need to know about. I just said this isn't the place or time to discuss it."

"I see," said Tobias, slightly disappointed. "Well, the doctors want to keep me here for a little while. Babysit me; you know how they are. I could get a paper cut, and they'd want to charge my health insurance as much as they possibly could. Speaking of which," almost casually, he questioned, "Is Bellwater Academy going to foot the bill for this? Am I covered under insurance?"

"Didn't you have insurance at Jefferson?"

"Yes, but do I need to remind you what happened with that?"

"You should still have your insurance."

"I'm presumed dead, Aurora. Speaking of being presumed dead, where is Mr. Ion?" Tobias was dimly aware that he had now gone off on two tangents in the last thirty seconds of this conversation, but he paid it no mind.

"Actually dead," Odion interjected. He didn't sound sorry to say this, and Tobias couldn't say he was sorry to hear it. "Took a fireball to the face. It seems Hunter struck him down."

"Hunter struck him down? But why? Hunter was working with him."

Odion shrugged. "You know the guy better than we do, Toby. Any ideas?"

"Several, actually. Each of them being more unlikely than the last."

"Most likely scenario?"

"Hunter threw a fireball at me and missed."

Tobias and Odion grinned at each other. Aurora

laughed.

"Well, that is one possibility, I suppose," she said, with a knowing glint in her eye. Tobias gave her a stink eye back.

"So what of the students? Lyra, Elena, and Darian? Did we find them?" Tobias asked.

"No sign of them," replied Aurora sadly. "Foxton and Finnian are in school today, though. It was a strange day at Bellwater Academy. With Percival gone, I am acting principal. It is…kind of nice, actually."

"Perfect! Because I need a job."

"You'll have one," she assured him.

"And what of the others? Sabrina, Matilda, Lucien, Agatha?"

"What about them?"

"Well, I assume they survived?"

"Oh yes, although they aren't too happy with me right now."

"Nor am I," Odion chimed in. "And we have good reason to be upset, Aurora."

"Yes, well, never mind that," Aurora dodged quickly as Tobias looked at her, a look of concern on his face. "We really should be going, Toby. We'll stop in and visit tomorrow, okay?"

"In person this time," Odion added. "These apparitions aren't the same."

Tobias nodded; he felt himself getting rather sleepy. "Alright, you two, leave me in peace then," he said. The two apparitions vanished into nothing, and Tobias was rocked to sleep by the dulcet tones of Kelly Clarkson.

Several hours later–or perhaps it was five minutes– Tobias awoke to the sound of his room door opening. Expecting the nurse, he simply said, "Good evening" without even opening his eyes.

"Good evening, Toby!"

Tobias's eyes sprang open. Standing in front of him was Hunter.

"Hunter!" Tobias began. "What are you doing here?" "I've

been ordered to kill you."

"I expected as much. This is, what, take three?"

"Not exactly. Before, I was ordered to bring you in. Capture you. Not this time. Now, the rebellion feels you need to be removed. Permanently."

The two men stood there for a minute, sizing each other up and down.

"Then why haven't you done so yet?" "Because

I don't want to."

Of all the reasons Tobias expected to hear out of Hunter's mouth, that was not it. "Because you don't want to?" he repeated, confused.

"I don't want to kill you, Toby. I still love you."

Tobias sighed. "Hunter, we've talked about this," he said slowly, with the air of explaining something to a small child. "I love you too, but not in a romantic sense. We were like brothers, we–"

"Why 'were,' Toby? We could still be like that."

"You attacked my school–"

"I had no idea you were in that school, Toby. I was following orders to abduct a handful of students–students whom the Bellwater Mages were eyeing up for recruitment."

"How do you know this?" asked Tobias suspiciously.

"There is a mole," provided Hunter. Tobias blinked at him. "Surprised? I suppose you should be."

"I'm less surprised that there is a mole, and more surprised that you're telling me about them, Hunter. Who is it?"

"Ah, see, that you're not getting out of me. Not yet, anyway."

"Well, it would be someone who would know the information I pass along to Aurora. So it's one of Sabrina, Lucien, Agatha, or Matilda. Or Odion, I suppose, though I don't think he'd know about that; he's still fairly new."

Hunter said nothing. He just stood there, looking at Tobias. He looked sad, defeated.

"Hunter," Tobias said gently. "We can still be friends. I know…I know you think we're something more, but…"

"But you do, too, Toby. I know you do."

Tobias hesitated. Then he explained, very slowly and deliberately, "Maybe I did at one point, Hunter. But not now. You left me, Hunter. You left me for a year and made no contact. Not once did you reach out, did you ask how I was doing, not once did you even bother to explain why you left."

"Would it have mattered?"

"To me, it would've."

"See, you say that, but I don't think you understand what that means, Toby. You made it very clear that you were choosing the Bellwater Mages over the Arcane Rebellion."

"I could say the same of you. You chose the rebellion over us. Why?"

Hunter didn't answer right away. He had started pacing around the room as though lost in thought. "Because," he said finally, "I think they have the right idea. Magic should be guarded and taught only to a select few. Not to just anyone who demonstrates potential. Those three students–Lyra, Elena, and Darian–they show real promise, Toby. Nice job with them. The other two–the fox and the fin kid–"

"Foxton and Finnian," Tobias corrected him.

"Whatever. I don't quite see what you see in them. An overconfident, stupid boy with his shy best friend?" "I

wouldn't expect you to understand, Hunter."

"Yes, well, that's not the only issue, Toby. Aurora!" "I

know the two of you have had your differences–" "--

that's putting it mildly–"

"--but if you gave her another chance, she could prove to you she's a great leader, Hunt."

"Yes, because strangling students with sunflowers and attacking police with earthquakes makes such a good, strong leader."

Tobias' heart sank. So, his suspicions had been confirmed.

"She lost control again?"

"It appears that way. Well, you talked to her, or her apparition anyway. They're all in hiding from the police, but it sounds like the police have decided to blame it on a natural disaster."

"She didn't say anything like that to me."

"Typical. Not telling the whole truth, expecting blind loyalty for nothing in return. Why do you give it to her, Toby?"

Tobias didn't answer. He stared into space for a hot minute, then eventually said, "I'm loyal. If that makes me an idiot, then so be it."

"You're not an idiot, Toby. But you are awfully naive sometimes."

The two men stared at each other in silence. It was a comfortable silence, though, like two old friends who hadn't seen each other for several months had gotten together for dinner and were just enjoying each other's company.

"So, are you going to kill me?" Tobias questioned eventually.

Hunter looked at him, examining him closely. Then he answered, "I haven't decided yet." And he teleported out of the room.

Chapter Sixteen:
Trials of Leadership

Due to an overabundance of pain medication, Tobias didn't remember much about his meeting with Hunter other than the very last thing the pair of them said to each other. Over the next few days, Tobias waited with bated breath in the hospital for Hunter to return. Tobias knew Hunter had a good heart, but he also knew Hunter could be unpredictable. While he was sure that Hunter was unlikely to follow through with the order to kill him (he didn't respond to orders very well), he also knew the Arcane Rebellion didn't take kindly to insubordination. He had known more than one of their agents who was met with an untimely demise for failing to follow through with an order to kill. The rebellion rarely captured their enemies; rather, they believed that only certain people could actually be converted to their cause. And once they ordered you killed, there was no going back: you were dead to them.

So it was with mixed emotions that Tobias left the hospital, discharged and ready for at-home healing, with Aurora and Odion by his side. He hadn't shared details about Hunter's visit with either of them; he felt Aurora would coddle him, and it would be too much trouble, and he wasn't sure how much he could trust Odion yet.

With Aurora's assistance, as Tobias was still rather

weak, the three of them drove back to the cottage.

"Well, Aurora. I believe there was something you wished to discuss with me once we made it back?" asked Tobias once they were settled in.

"That was no earthquake," It appeared Odion was bursting with this information. "Aurora killed those officers."

"You weren't even there, Odion!" Aurora snapped at him.

"Correct. I wasn't. I was helping Tobias!"

"So, you don't know what may or may not have gone down."

"What really happened, Aurora?"

Aurora sighed and looked at Tobias. This was so typical of him; he was always trusting her, always willing to hear out her explanations. This time, however, she felt her explanation was less than satisfactory. She really did feel guilty for what she had done, but it was the only option that presented itself to her at the time. And she stood by that.

"After you and Odion teleported to the hospital, we surrounded Hunter. Percival was already dead when we arrived on the scene, seemingly from Hunter himself. I tied Hunter up with vines—a personal favorite spell of mine, as you know. Sabrina hit him with an Anti-Teleportation Spell, so he couldn't get away. Then we began walking him to the cottage; we couldn't teleport there due to

Sabrina's spell, which was necessary to prevent his escape."

"But we encountered a problem. The police found us, and Hunter made it seem as though we were kidnapping him. We were surrounded by police, and they pulled their firearms on us, Toby. I did what I felt I had to, to get us out of there. I didn't want to, and I took no pleasure in it. I hope you realize that."

The three of them sat there in silence. It felt like a long while until anyone said anything, though it was less than five minutes. Then, Tobias turned to Odion.

"Did you ask her about this a few days ago? Did she explain all this to you?"

"Er…not exactly. Tell you the truth, Toby, Aurora and I haven't exactly been talking much as of late."

"I see," He said. He appeared to be lost in thought.

Aurora stared at him, and after yet another five minutes, she blurted out, "So what are you thinking, Toby?"

Tobias didn't answer right away. He took a drink of his water, then said very slowly and deliberately, as if he weighed every word. "I think you did what you thought you had to, Aurora. I don't know what I would have done in your situation. I'm happy you and the others are safe. That's all that matters to me."

Aurora beamed at him.

"How do the others feel about this?" His question was directed not at her, but at Odion.

"There has been...discussion...that perhaps Aurora should be removed from her leadership position."

Aurora frowned at Odion. "Why didn't you tell me about this sooner?"

"Because I agree with them, to be frank."

"Were you the one who started this...discussion?" "No,

ma'am. I'm not sure who it was. But, frankly, everyone thinks so. Well, everyone except Agatha." "I

see."

Aurora sat back in her chair, deflated.

"Has anything like this ever happened before?" questioned Odion.

"No, not like this," said Aurora. "I mean, I believe there have been...whispers...in the past. But nothing like this. And I hate to say it, but perhaps the others have a point."

"Then why don't we have a meeting about it? We can have the others here on Saturday?" asked Tobias.

"That's a good idea," she agreed. She smiled at Tobias, and he grinned at her. She turned to Odion, who didn't look nearly as happy about this as Tobias did.

"And…what if the meeting doesn't go your way, Aurora?"

"Then I will step down, and someone else can take over."

"Like whom?"

Aurora thought for a minute. Agatha was still recovering from her broken hip. Tobias was recovering from his gunshot, and he'd never agree to it. Odion was far too new, and if he openly admitted to her that he agreed she was unfit to be a leader, he didn't want to recommend him. That left Sabrina, Lucien, or Matilda.

"Matilda," she said finally. "She'll give me the fairest chance out of all of them."

"Then it's settled. We'll recommend Matilda temporarily take over as leader of the Bellwater Mages," said Tobias. He stood up and limped over to the kitchen. "Who's hungry?"

They enjoyed a delicious dinner of pork chops and mashed potatoes. Over dinner, the three of them talked about the goings-on at Bellwater Academy. With the loss of Percival Ion, Aurora had taken over as an interim principal. Odion had returned to the school as a math teacher, and his long-term sub had taken over Aurora's guidance counselor position.

There was also discussion happening among the school board about making Aurora's appointment to the principal position a permanent thing. Tobias found this very interesting; Aurora had never shared with him principal aspirations, but Aurora expressed a newfound interest in taking on this role.

"Think of how much easier it would be if I were the principal! We could make real changes and prioritize magical education."

"Yes, but if you have Matilda take over as leader of our group, Aurora, wouldn't that undermine your authority a bit?"

Aurora thought for a moment, then replied, "I don't think so. I think it would be good for the leader of our group and the principal of our school to be two different people."

"I suppose that makes sense," Odion said, shrugging. He didn't really care one way or the other about what happened. He was content in his role as a math teacher.

They ate in silence for the next quarter hour. Then Odion bid them goodnight and returned to his own home. Tobias and Aurora stayed up. They talked for a little over an hour about things like the weather and school before eventually—

"Are you really willing to let Matilda replace you, Aurora?"

Aurora didn't answer at once. She sipped from her coffee cup a few times before finally answering, "Temporarily, yes. If the group feels it is time for a fresh face in that position, I will allow her to take over on a short-term basis. If it goes well, then perhaps I would allow it to continue more long-term. But if not…well, we will see."

They went to bed shortly after that interaction. The two of them spent the next few days mostly on their own; Aurora had school, and Tobias was still recovering from being shot, so he was spending most of his time sleeping and relaxing around the house.

Finally, Saturday came. Agatha, Odion, Matilda, Sabrina, and Lucien entered the cottage. Agatha seemed like she was making tremendous headway in her recovery; she was barely using her cane and seemed able to walk much longer without needing to stop and rest.

The group was talking happily about the changes Aurora had made as principal in the short time it had been since she had taken over for Percival when Tobias entered the room.

"Tobias!" greeted Lucien. He seemed surprised to see him. "I…well, it's good to see you! I wasn't sure you were going to recover. How are you doing?"

"I'm doing well, thanks, Lucien," said Tobias, smiling at him. "A bullet is never a good thing, but I seem to be recovering just fine."

Lucien nodded. "Well, if there's anything you need, don't hesitate to ask."

Tobias thanked him and sat down. When Matilda greeted Tobias and everyone's attention turned towards them, Lucien made eye contact with Sabrina, and the two shared a meaningful look.

A look that Aurora happened to notice. It made her very uneasy, though she didn't say anything.

"Alright, everyone. I'd like to get this meeting started." She called the meeting to order, and everyone sat down in the same places they'd sat last time.

"Now, as we know, there have been some…recent developments that I think merit discussion. I think we should start," she took a deep breath, "with the conversations that have supposedly been happening behind my back about my ability as a leader for the Bellwater Mages."

The group sat in silence, staring at her.

"Aurora…" Sabrina began, but Aurora cut her off.

"Listen! I am not unreasonable. I know that what I did, killing all those police officers, I know that was…not ideal, to say the least. But I also know that if I hadn't done that, we'd be imprisoned right now, or dead. They'd find out about our powers and torture and kill us. I don't want that to happen. And I'm sure you don't want that to happen either."

Tobias nodded encouragingly. Aurora gained a little courage at his support. She looked around the room and was delighted to find that Agatha also seemed to agree with her words; she nodded at her to continue. Even Odion, who Aurora knew was not her biggest fan, seemed to be giving her the benefit of the doubt.

"So, is there a discussion?"

"Yes," said Sabrina. She seemed to have been preparing a speech; she stood up and addressed the group. "Several of us have felt that your leadership has been disturbingly…well, 'uneven,' I guess, for lack of a better word. And the massacre of police officers is not our only concern. It has come to our attention that you were the one to drive out the students Lyra, Elena, and Darian by attacking them with magic."

Aurora froze. How could Sabrina possibly know about this?

"I don't think we can trust you, Aurora," Lucien chimed in. "I think if you're going to go around and attack students for expressing concerns or different opinions from you, what will you do to us if we do the same?" he looked uncomfortable speaking up, and looked to Sabrina for support. She nodded at him, smiling.

"I think the two of you are being a little unfair to Aurora," Tobias said. He didn't stand up, though he did sit up a little straighter. The group turned to face him. "Aurora has done a lot for our group. I think we've all had moments where we've lost control of our magic; I know I've had my fair share of it."

"Yes, Tobias, but you've never attacked anyone with magic because you've been so upset. Aurora's done it twice in less than forty-eight hours now. Has anyone else lost control of their magic and attacked an innocent person?"

Tobias frowned, then said slowly, "I want to make it crystal clear that I do not condone Aurora's recent actions. I am speaking more about past events. She took over our group from a leader who wanted to declare war on the non-magical people, at great personal risk to herself. She confronted and killed him. Per our bylaws, that gives her the right to lead us. She has helped prevent me from committing suicide on more than one occasion. She has helped Agatha," he nodded at the old woman, "overcome a drinking problem, if I recall correctly. She has given us many, many chances. We have all made mistakes here. And to answer your question, Sabrina: Yes, I have lost control of my magic and attacked someone. Perhaps not to the point that Aurora has. But I have."

No one spoke, stood up, or raised their hands. It seemed the others in the group–Odion, Agatha, Matilda– didn't want to voice an opinion. Tobias looked at Odion, and they made eye contact. Odion, however, shook his head: it seemed as though he could not support Aurora, despite his friendship with Tobias.

"I have to agree," Agatha blurted out. The group turned to look at her. "Aurora's been our leader for years and has never had a problem. If she's willing to seek help for her anger, then we should give her the benefit of the doubt. But listen carefully, Aurora. If you don't seek help, and you continue to make rash decisions, I will make sure there's new leadership put into place." Agatha looked at Aurora sternly.

Aurora nodded at her. "Understood, Agatha."

Sabrina sat down and smiled at Agatha. "I'm sorry, Agatha. I just don't agree with your statement. I think it would be best for someone else to take over leadership duties. Especially as Aurora is now also interim principal."

There was, once again, silence in the room among the mages. Sabrina and Lucien, it seemed, were intent upon taking leadership away from Aurora. Tobias and Agatha had voiced support for Aurora. Per their bylaws, Aurora was not to be given a vote here. That left the decision to Odion and Matilda.

Tobias glanced at Odion, looking somewhat desperate.

However, Matilda stood.

"I have to agree with Sabrina and Lucien," she said calmly. "Aurora, you have too much on your plate. Let one of us help you, especially as you navigate your new position at the school."

That was settled. Even if Odion voiced support for Odion, it would be a tie, and a tie would result in a new leader. Aurora sighed, then said, "May I recommend Matilda for leadership then?"

"Oh, no," said Matilda quickly. "I don't want it. I think Sabrina should take it."

She took a glance at Sabrina, who smiled widely at her.

"I'd be honored to take the role, Matilda," she said, sweetly. She stood up at once; power radiated from her, and the room felt like the temperature increased ten degrees. "Aurora, did you have any other business to discuss at tonight's meeting?"

"No, I don't," said Aurora. She was looking at Sabrina suspiciously, though the others seemed not to notice.

"Very well. I think we can adjourn this meeting for tonight, everyone. It's been a long day. We will have a union meeting later this week, assuming, of course, that's okay with our principal?"

"Shouldn't be a problem," said Aurora.

Chapter Seventeen:
Love Hurts

Tobias left the cottage shortly after the meeting with the other teachers. He bid adieu to them, promising to return later that evening. As was his custom, he needed a minute to himself. He needed to think, to ponder. He didn't notice Sabrina and Lucien huddled together, watching him walk towards the clearing in the forest, voices in frantic whispers.

He began walking to his favorite spot: the clearing in the woods. As he walked, he thought about everything he had accomplished and everything that had happened to him in the last few weeks. Saving the students. Bringing them to Bellwater. Subbing for Agatha O'Connor. Getting fired by Percival Ion. Taking a trip with Odion to an Arcane Rebellion stronghold. Getting shot by his old principal. And having Hunter meet up with him in his hospital room.

This sounds like a melodrama, he thought bitterly. How could one person have this much crap happen to them?

He walked until he reached the clearing, then sat down on the cold grass. It was chilly, so he pulled a blanket out of his hiding spot (a hole under the rock) and cuddled up with it by the water. It was nice to get away from everything and everyone, just for a minute.

He laid back and looked up at the stars. There wasn't a cloud in sight, and the moon was rather dim that night, so the stars could be made out perfectly. He was never much of a stargazer; he didn't know any of the constellations, but he still enjoyed looking up at them. He often wondered what else there was to life. Surely there was more to life than whatever this planet held for them?

Tobias sighed. He had often had these thoughts and feelings that perhaps it would be better if he had perished, or just ended his life. But that was impossible. You couldn't kill yourself with your own magic, no matter how hard you tried. Tobias could call forth seven hundred bolts of lightning to strike him all at one time, and it wouldn't kill him. Another mage could potentially kill you with their magic, if they specialized in an element different from your own. But Tobias had too much pride to ever allow that to happen.

Aurora always yelled at him whenever he expressed these thoughts and feelings. He recalled a specific instance where she outright told him that he wasn't disposable like he seemed to think he was. He supposed she loved him, and it was hard for her to think about his death. But he wasn't sure if it was him she truly loved, or just his uncanny ability to control the elements.

Tobias sat around the clearing for a long while, alone with his thoughts. He enjoyed being alone, especially after the events of the last several weeks. It was hard to imagine that it had been mere weeks since he had saved Foxton and Finnian, and Lyra, Elena, and Darian. He thought about the latter three, where they were, how they were doing. He thought they must have been very hurt and angry over Aurora's actions. He supposed he couldn't blame them; Aurora had a very distinct personality that was sometimes hard to get along with. Not to mention, she had practically killed one of them because of a flippant teenage comment.

He also thought about Odion, who had been disgruntled with Aurora as well. He liked Odion, though he did sometimes feel Odion was a bit too immature for his taste. Though, to be fair to him, he also didn't know Aurora nearly as well as Tobias did.

There was a sound behind Tobias. He jumped up quickly, ready for action. A tall, ginger boy with freckles was walking towards him: Foxton.

"Good evening, Foxton," Tobias said briskly. "What are you doing out here?"

"Out for a walk, Mr. T," Foxton replied casually. He looked around the clearing, and his eyes focused on Tobias' blanket that was lying on the ground. "Are you...er...homeless? Sleeping out here?"

"No. Well, I guess technically, I am, in that I don't have a house of my own. But I always have a room to sleep in if I need it."

Foxton nodded. "So, is Aurora your girlfriend or something?"

Tobias frowned. He had not expected to be discussing his love life with a student. A former student, it was true, but it was still kind of awkward. "Er…no, she's not."

It was not unusual for Foxton to be nosy and overly talkative, though Tobias wouldn't pretend it didn't irritate him sometimes. While it was true that Foxton and Finnian had been two of his favorites, Foxton could also be a bit much for him.

"So, Foxton, you just strode out for a walk and stumbled in here, eh? Have you been here before? Other than the time I brought you here, I mean."

"Nope, haven't been back," he replied. He looked around the clearing, and then his face fell slightly. "I think," he said slowly, "it's just starting to dawn on me how much I lost a few weeks ago, Mr. T. My parents. My friends. My job. I lost it all to that fire. And it's surreal that now I'm learning how to use magic, too. If I had had this training, then…would I have been able to stop it?"

These were dangerous words that Foxton was saying to Tobias, and he immediately intervened.

"Listen, Foxton! What happened wasn't your fault. There's nothing you could have done about it; there's nothing you did that caused it." He hesitated for a moment, then said, "The people who did it are…misguided. I'm not excusing what they did, or their actions. But you are not responsible for them."

"You're gonna find them and kill them, right, Mr. T?"

Tobias shifted uncomfortably at this question. So, he used one of his favorite tactics: deflect.

"I believe I told you to call me Tobias."

"You did, but you'll always be Mr. T or Mr. Thornfield to me, Mr. T. I would never call a teacher of mine their first name."

Tobias rolled his eyes at Foxton.

"Sorry! I respect you too much to use your first name. Now, back to my question. That tactic of yours isn't going to work on me."

Tobias didn't answer right away. He was thinking hard. It was obvious Foxton wanted him to answer "Yes" to this question, but…could he? Could he give his word he would kill Hunter?

"I…don't know, Foxton," he said finally. "It's complicated."

"How so?"

"You wouldn't understand."

"I understand my family and friends are dead because of the Arcane Rebellion. What else is there to understand?"

"Plenty," said Tobias firmly. "But you wouldn't understand it, you're—"

"Too young? Please. I'm almost eighteen years old; I think I can handle it."

"Turning eighteen doesn't make you an adult."

"What are you talking about? I'll have my own ID, I'll be able to vote, and register for military service. How am I not an adult?"

"You're an adult in the eyes of the law. But you're not really an adult at eighteen. You still have a lot to learn."

"Would you say you still have a lot to learn, Mr. T?"

"Yes, I would. I'll never stop learning."

"Then teach me! I don't care if you don't think I'll understand, Mr. T. Teach me why this is complicated. Help me to understand!"

"Have you ever loved anyone, Foxton?"

Foxton blinked at this question. Then he said, "Well, yeah. My parents, and my friends, I suppose. My family."

"Of course you loved your family, and your friends. Would you do anything for them? Would you go to the ends of the earth for them? Would you stay up until four in the morning talking to them on the phone? Would you drive fifteen hundred miles to help them in a crisis?"

Foxton looked uncomfortable at Tobias's questions.

Then he said, "Yeah, maybe, I guess. If I had to." "See, you've loved, you've been loved, but you've never truly loved until you meet someone that you would do all of those things and more for. Unquestioningly, unwaveringly. There are many people in this world whom I love, Foxton. And…one of those people happens to be part of the Arcane Rebellion."

They stood, staring at each other in complete silence. Then Foxton asked, very quietly, "Would you say you love me, Mr. T?"

Tobias turned away from Foxton at this question. He had not expected it, and truthfully, he didn't know how to answer it. "I love you just like I would any of my students, Foxton. I will help you to be the best version of you as you can be."

"That wasn't what I asked. Would you do those things for me? Stay up till four in the morning, travel fifteen hundred miles to help me out of a crisis?"

Tobias didn't answer. He stared deep into the pond, thinking hard. How could he answer? He couldn't tell Foxton—one of his students—that he'd do those things, even if he would. The annoying thing about Tobias, or so he thought about himself, was he trusted entirely too much in the goodness of people. It was rather irritating to deal with, feeling like he had to go through the motions to help others feel loved when he himself didn't feel loved.

After a few minutes, Foxton sighed and said, "Okay, Mr. T., I get it. I'll leave you to...whatever you're doing."

Tobias turned and looked at him; Foxton was walking away towards the path. Tobias opened his mouth to speak.

Then, fire rained down upon the clearing. Pure, unfiltered fire struck both Tobias and Foxton hard. Foxton screamed in pain and surprise, running towards a nearby tree. Tobias made a motion with his fist towards the pond; water soared up overhead and stopped the flames. The water from the pond swirled around, forming a cloudlike shape overhead. Water droplets started to pour down on the clearing like rain, covering both Tobias and Foxton.

"Foxton!" cried Tobias. "Foxton, are you alright?!"

"Yeah, I think so," Foxton gasped, struggling to his feet.

"Tobias!"

Hunter teleported into the clearing, away from the now pouring rain that soaked the ground and trees around Tobias and Hunter. He was on the other side, and he was not smiling, nor did he give any indication he was happy. Quite the opposite.

"I've made my decision, Tobias. Just as you've made yours. It is time for you to go."

Hunter made fire appear out of thin air; he twisted and turned the fire in midair with his hands, and it quickly took the form of an arrow. Not needing a bow, he used magic to shoot the fiery arrow directly into the clearing. Tobias put a protective barrier around himself, expecting it to go for him. But it soared right past him, and with a scream, Tobias realized, too late, that Hunter's true target had been–

"Foxton!"

Tobias turned and ran towards his student. The arrow had pierced directly above his heart; Foxton had avoided death by inches. Foxton was gasping for air, the fire starting to seep into his skin. Tobias grabbed him; he was piping hot to the touch. Tobias swore; using his own magic, icy cold water appeared out of nowhere and soaked Foxton. Foxton gasped and struggled to breathe, but Tobias kept the water going; if Foxton couldn't breathe for a few seconds, that wouldn't be the end of the world, but if he burned to death, that would be terrible. Tobias's water had healing properties when used against magical injuries, and Foxton's skin—which before had turned a nasty charred black—was starting to go back to its white, pale, normal self.

A ball of fire exploded directly behind Tobias. Tobias went flying away from Foxton and slammed into a tree a solid twenty feet away from the boy. Hunter laughed.

"Your biggest weakness has always been your uncanny need to help out everyone around you, Tobias! You put others first and put yourself at risk. Haven't you heard the phrase, 'Put your own mask on before helping others'?"

Hunter launched a second ball of fire directly at Tobias. Tobias snapped his fingers at the cloud of water overhead; it immediately turned into a full-on thunderstorm, flying towards Hunter with alarming speed. Rain, wind, and thunder immediately started striking Hunter, who was blown backward by the force of the storm. The storm followed him; it seemed that Tobias had made hurting Hunter the storm's personal mission. Hunter teleported away from the storm, standing directly next to Foxton.

"No!" Tobias shrieked. He launched a gust of wind directly at the duo; Foxton was blown directly into the storm. Tobias waved his hands, and the storm shifted priority. Instead of attacking Hunter, it sealed Foxton off into a powerful cloud that surrounded him with water, wind, and lightning. Hunter had teleported before crashing into a tree and found himself directly behind Tobias. Tobias didn't have time to move before a second fireball came soaring at him.

"No–Mr. T!" Foxton cried out.

Tobias teleported away at the last second. The fireball crashed directly into the cloud holding Foxton. The water from the cloud immediately disintegrated the fireball. Tobias reappeared where he had started: by the rock outside the pond. He launched a bolt of lightning at Hunter, which missed him by inches and instead hit the tree next to him. The tree immediately crashed to the ground. Hunter, standing directly beneath the tree, screamed as the tree fell on top of him. He lay unconscious, possibly dead, under the tree.

Tobias instantly turned towards Foxton.

"Foxton, listen to me! I'm sending you back to your safe house."

"No, Mr. T! What about you?"

"I can take care of myself, I pro–"

A fiery arrow pierced Tobias in the square of his back.

Tobias gasped and turned around.

Hunter was standing in the clearing, and Tobias realized something: he was completely unharmed. He had used an apparition to do his fighting for him.

"How did you—?"

Tobias didn't finish his question. He turned back to Foxton.

"I'm...sending you back now, Foxton."

"No, Mr. T! Fight back!"

A second fiery arrow struck Tobias in the buttock. Tobias shrieked in pain, then waved his hands. Instantly, the cloud started to collapse. A black hole was starting to form underneath Foxton.

"That hole...will take you to your safe house. Go into it, Foxton!"

"No!"

A third fiery arrow launched itself and struck Tobias' kneecap. He fell to the ground, panting.

"I said go, Foxton!"

A gust of wind forced Foxton down into the hole. He fought it, fought it with all his might. But the wind was too powerful; he blew backward and out of sight. A split second later, Tobias collapsed, and the black hole disappeared. The cloud, wind, water, and lightning ceased to fight against Hunter; the water dropped where it stood, flooding the ground rather than returning to the pond. For

Tobias didn't have time to send it back to its source.

Hunter teleported directly to Tobias and felt his face. Tobias was warm, unconscious, and not quite dead. Hunter collapsed onto the ground next to Tobias, tears streaming down his face.

"Toby!" he whispered in anguish. He seemed to be full of regret. "I'm sorry, Toby! I won't let anything happen to you. I promise!"

Chapter Eighteen:
A New Beginning

Hunter wrapped Tobias's unconscious body up into a warm embrace. Tobias was still alive, but only just. Hunter had a plan to keep his friend safe. For he wouldn't kill him. He couldn't. He would tell Sabrina and Lucien that he had done it, but he would be keeping Tobias alive. Even if it cost him everything.

Hunter teleported the two men away from the clearing where they had dueled and appeared back at Jefferson High School, which was in the process of being rebuilt. The community was grieving. This was certainly going to be the last place Aurora or any of the Bellwater Mages would think to look for Tobias. Sabrina and Lucien certainly wouldn't look here. He doubted whether they would even realize that Tobias used to teach here.

Hunter turned away from the construction site and towards a small house that he knew to be vacant. He had recently acquired this house; the couple that had just purchased it had been teachers at Jefferson High, and their will had left him the sole beneficiary of their house. They had no family to fight him for this property, and even if they did, he had done everything properly. His friend Ted had been an attorney prior to joining the Arcane Rebellion, and still completed legal tasks for the Rebellion on occasion.

Hunter entered the house. The house, and the acre of land it sat on, was enchanted to prevent teleportation. The house was empty except for a small supply of food and water, and several chains attached to the wall.

Hunter sat Tobias down on the floor and leaned him up against the wall. It had taken a lot out of him to teleport the two of them to this location, then to walk them to the house. He was exhausted as he chained Tobias up.

The chains—which he stole from the rebellion—were enchanted to drain the occupant of the ability to use magic. Of course, this would happen naturally over the course of time; magic could only be performed if one felt loved, connected, and valued. Tobias was to be cut off from everyone and everything he loved. Everyone and everything except, of course, for Hunter. And if Tobias didn't love him anymore, then he just wouldn't feel love. This would prevent him from being able to cast magic.

It was fool proof, thought Hunter savagely. Tobias would be forced to either fall in love with him, or he would have to spend the rest of his life locked up in this house with no one for company except for Hunter. Hunter didn't have visitors, and he certainly wouldn't start now. He had what he needed.

Once Tobias was properly secured to the chains, Hunter went over and grabbed a small bottle of water from the stack of supplies. He poured it over Tobias, who woke up, groaning in pain.

"Wake up, Toby. Welcome home."

Tobias opened his eyes and made out Hunter in the darkness.

"Hunter..?"

"Yeah, babe. Don't worry, we're safe now."

Tobias went to stand up but was unable to do so because of the chains. He fell back over, landing hard on his stomach as he did so. He grunted; that was where he had had surgery a week ago.

"Don't move too much, Toby. Conserve your strength."

Tobias looked around the room. Then he noticed his chains.

"Hunter...what did you do?"

"It's a precaution, Toby. Can't have you getting any ideas about leaving me again, right?"

Tobias stared at Hunter as though he had never seen him before.

"Er...Hunter, are you okay?"

"I've never been better," said Hunter proudly, grinning at Tobias. "I was ordered to kill you, but I couldn't do it, so I brought you here instead! If I leave you here, I can tell the others that I completed my mission. They'll never know. Your group of mages will fall, and the Arcane Rebellion will take over." He thought for a minute, then he whispered to Tobias, "and we'll get to be together still.

It'll be like I never left."

"Hunter," Tobias began, but quickly doubled over in pain. Hunter frowned at him.

"No, Toby. Conserve your strength. You're injured and need to rest."

"Foxton…"

Hunter rolled his eyes. "The kid's fine, he's with that Odion dunderhead."

He waved his hand in a fluidlike motion. On the surface of the floor, where the water Hunter had poured on Tobias lay, a shimmering image of a ginger-haired boy with freckles talking frantically to a young, well-dressed man and a middle-aged woman appeared in front of Tobias' eyes.

"Foxton…Odion…Aurora…"

"You see? They're fine. I didn't touch them."

"But what will you do to them? Now that I'm out of the way?"

Tobias tried to get up again, but quickly sank back down. Hunter stood up and turned away from him, walking slowly towards the front door.

"They chose the wrong side, Toby, and must pay for their crimes. You chose the wrong side too. But I'm giving you a reprieve."

"Where are we, Hunter?"

"We're about a mile away from your old school, Jefferson High."

Tobias was struggling, gasping for air. The injuries he had sustained as a result of his battle with Hunter were starting to take their toll on him.

"Hunter, please…please. I'll do anything. Please…don't hurt…them."

Tobias' pleading made Hunter stop. "I want you to love me again."

Hunter said the words so softly, so quietly that he thought for a moment that Tobias hadn't heard him. But Tobias replied less than a minute later.

"I never stopped."

"Then why do you care about them so much, Toby?"

Hunter turned around and faced Tobias.

"Because…I love them too, Hunter. You can love more than one person, you know."

"They don't love you. Don't you see that they're hurting you?"

"No, Hunter. The only one hurting me is you. And I'm not just talking about the last…what, hour? The last year. You broke my heart. You ghosted me. And Aurora had to pick up the pieces. She finally did, I finally got myself to a good place. And then you do this, Hunter. Yeah, I still love you. But I'm mad as hell at you right now!"

Hunter stared at Tobias, unsure of what to think. Then he finally said, "You'll thank me for this someday," and walked out of the house.

About the Author

Denis James was born and raised in the Duluth, Minnesota area. When not teaching others in his day job, Denis enjoys reading, writing, anything Pokémon, and the occasional television series marathon. His other hobbies include traveling and spending time at the family cabin.

Connect with Denis James:

- Facebook: Denis James – Writer
- Instagram: denisjameswriter
- Twitter: denisjameswrite
- Patreon: Denis James – Writer

Made in the USA
Monee, IL
20 July 2025